wretched and the beautiful ways we love, we let go, and we hold on, to our sorrow. Above all it is a diary of our time, as we wrestle with the question of what it means to be human and what it means to be other. Perhaps CATACLYSM is horror, perhaps it is science fiction, perhaps it is literary fiction, but it is in any incarnation an excoriation of our impulses, of what drives us and of how we lie to ourselves.

"No spoilers, but I do feel compelled to say this: Dearie, you are wrong. You may be the most human of us all. I did save for myself one line, which is heartbreakingly relevant in its immediacy: '[People] fight only what they can see, which is each other.'
If only we could grow into something more than people."

— Cassondra Windwalker, author of *Idle Hands* and *What Hides in the Cupboards*

"*Cataclysm* by Tiffany Meuret is marvelous. Packed with observations about love, power, obsession, societal collapse, and the bond between mothers and their children, it will both entertain you and give you plenty to think about. It is alarmingly easy to see how our world could follow the trajectory that Meuret's world has traversed; if only more people would read more books like this, perhaps we might finally learn a thing or two, both about our society and about ourselves."

— Laura Morrison, author of *How to Break an Evil Curse*

Also by Tiffany Meuret

Little Bird

A Flood of Posies

CATACLYSM

TIFFANY MEURET

Denver, Colorado

Published in the United States by:
Spaceboy Books LLC
1627 Vine Street
Denver, CO 80206
www.readspaceboy.com

Cover includes CC0 images from Image by Alexander Antropov, Thomas G., and Wolfgang Eckert from Pixabay

ISBN: 978-1-951393-32-8
First printed April 2024

To the demons I exorcised while writing this book

ONE

A mother and her child escape an incoming blast, sprinting toward the desert to shelter in its vastness. Calcified earth pulverizes their shins as they run and run and run, legs pumping until the heat grips their lungs in a vice. They are not meant to run like this anymore; they are not scurrying rats anymore—they are burrowing things, possums, concocting mazes just out of sight. No one ever saw them coming until the last moment, but a moment is all a fox needs.

The son buckles, collapsing to the dirt, the mother sheltering her child from the sun with her body. He is a man now, but she still rubs the wiry hair on the back of his scalp like she did when he was a child, telling him it would be okay. They have run far enough. The son cries into his hands, mud smearing on the apples of his cheeks as he furiously wipes away tears. He says he is sorry. The mother says nothing back.

She thinks to herself that at least they tried. She and her son are the flares into a black sky as the ship sinks, bright, furious, captivating, fleeting in their power, yet still enough to get the world to look up. Everyone is looking up at their private patch of the sky now, searching for a missile the mother knows is coming for her.

She wishes she had her gun. The way her child weeps is unbearable. She wants to send him to sleep before it comes, before the blast renders his flesh to charcoal, sealing his final moments as a comfort in his mother's arms, not a searing flash of pain, not a misplaced comeuppance written by her hand. She can't bear the guilt she has bloomed into his soul, the way it has ruined him; she ruined him, her boy, she destroyed him. But she has no gun, dropped it in the scramble, screaming to run, for everyone to run, to get the fuck out of here, their homes, their lives. Everything they'd managed to scrap together was mere moments from annihilation. Again. Run before it gets you too.

Jets whip into a frenzy above them. The mother gazes up, still stroking her child's hair, marveling at it, the creature she created.

The child presses his nails into his mother's skin, drawing blood, wishing to burrow back inside her just as all the sound in the world sucks away by a terrible weapon colliding with its target.

PART ONE

THE WOMAN

SEPTEMBER 24TH, 2024

There is no better time to start a journal than the end of the world. I figure that's generally when all human beings begin to write—some sort of ending. That's what I'm doing. I'm writing to no one. To me. To whoever finds this, if this journal is meant to be found. It doesn't matter if the pages survive. I hope they do because that means there is someone out there to read them.

The end started all cozy-like. Still feels cozy. Such a stupid word, cozy, and yet that's where I land every time I think about it. My children are playing in the backyard as I write this—giggling, fighting, jumping on the trampoline that has caused so many injuries over the years. They know something is wrong, but not enough to know how badly and swiftly the tide is turning. We won't be able to stay here much longer. I guess about a year. My dad assumes more. He thinks I'm being dramatic. I am not. He is just too delusional to see clearly.

We are all sick with worry, but who isn't? My parents live down the block but visit daily. Dad says to let them come, them meaning that vague otherness of the enemy. Let them bomb the house. He refuses to move anyway, so might as well get it over with (he says). Mom walks aimlessly between our two houses to try and occupy her anxiety. I tell her to stop traveling alone, but she won't listen. The mob is still a distant thing. The Mob^{tm}. We live in suburbia, sheltered just enough to think the inner city a different country, yet not enough to actually stay safe. They are coming, and they will either catch us, kill us, or make us one of them.

But the mob, the amorphous thing that it is, is lumbering and dumb. It will not see me coming, I'll make sure of that. The worry I feel, the terror of everything, the unknown, the distress, the sadness and loss peppering our future does not deter me. Finally, I think.

Finally, I can be the murderous bitch I've always wanted to be.

~The Woman

OCTOBER 2ND, 2024

The family lives with me now. All of us. My parents, my siblings, and their spouses. My children no longer play outside. Anarchy from top to bottom, and yet still things are quiet. The mob was crushed with an authoritarian fist—the fringes flung against the floorboards like blood spatter. Just give them time. They will be back, and more of them, and now with an axe to grind.

Everyone has guns. The police, what remain, have the most, but they are easily swarmed, choked, and stripped. The iron fist that crushed the first insurrection crumbled to dust shortly after. To think only a week has passed since my last entry.

I don't know what to do. I want to know what to do. I pretend to know, even. My kids and family look at me like the matriarch, or else I just assume they do. I absorb the pressure without being asked. I'm not sure what to do with all their focused attention. There is no reassuring, which is a relief. I hate having to tell people it will be okay. The sentiment sounds so hollow, and now everyone else understands that it is. Nothing is okay because okay was the old baseline. It will be quite some time before we create another one. Perhaps not even in my lifetime. I can only pray for my kids.

D.C. is quiet. Congress remotes in and accomplishes nothing. Nuclear war is on the lips of everyone, a reactionary impulse, our greatest united fear. We are a giant toddler missing the bottle, one wrong move and it ends for everyone. Dad used to say that should nuclear war come, he hoped the first bomb landed on top of his head. I thought it disturbing and macabre as a kid, but now, he was right on the money. He is the quietest of all of us now. I don't know how long he will last in this directionless world.

The neighborhood convenes at night. They think it will be easier to spot an incoming mob in the dark. They assume they'll come with torches. Fucking dementedly stupid. My god. But at least they convene and watch. Mentions of perimeters and fencing are bubbling. A good idea for protection, bad idea for everything else—food, medical care, even water. Who knows how long the faucets will run? Municipal water is the greatest weapon of the powerful now. Money clings to its illusion, but that will fade soon. We keep it, but not as much as the others, piling their paper money under their mattresses as if it will last them through the winter, to emerge into the new old world as if nothing ever happened. They say they're keeping their money safe. From what? The mob? They don't want it. The government? They don't need it.

I'm having the kids fill water jugs to keep them busy. They think it's fun. I let them play in it, while it still runs. Today may be the last day they can.

~The Woman

OCTOBER 30TH, 2024

FUCK.
FUCK FUCK FUCK.

I hate this shit. I don't want to live like this. I hate this shit and I want it to be over. My sister got a migraine and I didn't have the medicine she needed. The kids were loud, as if sensing the mood in the home and deciding it was in everyone's best interest to make it worse. Dad left the house two hours ago looking for Diet Pepsi, citing "bullshit" as good enough reason to brave the city. Mom stares out the front window because Dad refused to let her come. He didn't take his phone with him. Phones are a hot commodity now, and getting caught with one is worse than getting stuck without one.

I want to watch my shows, my stupid bullshit shows. I want to eat my kids Halloween candy without them knowing. I want to worry about money for Christmas and finding a good plumber for the steady drip of the master bathroom faucet. I want to waste hours searching online listings for houses I can't afford. I fucking hate this. This dread is a snake and it's killing me. My kids are smiling yet miserable. They lie like the rest of us. We are drowning, and we are not prepared.

~The Woman

DECEMBER 15TH, 2024

Shit moves fast in the apocalypse. Well, actually, it is rather slow until it isn't. Boring until you're running for your life. There was a moment of hope a little while ago, just a glimmer. We heard loudspeakers. Thought it was the cops. Never have I ever thought I'd relish the thought of a stampede of cops marching up my block, but then again, the end of civility really puts a craving for order in one's belly, no matter how cruel. Anyway, they came once and only once. The entire family bum-rushed the front window. We'd been about to board it up when we heard it. Police. They'd organized, we thought. They were coming to regain power. Fine. Great. Anything to return to a new normal. We didn't even care if they punished us. I would have personally kissed their boots if it would have made any difference.

But relief was short lived. I should have known better. What a drug hope is—makes even the cleverest of us high on our own farts. I should have known.

My brother knew it wasn't real. I snapped at him, but he knew.

The dreaded 'mob' was swamped and executed the second they crossed our shanty threshold. The neighborhood watch waited a few hours, then days, then a week, for reinforcements. Retaliation. But none came. I went poking around after the house was asleep. Someone made a pile of their bodies in the cul-de-sac a few streets down. Nary a blade in sight. Nothing but a slicked-up gang with a megaphone.

We had to leave. There would only be more. Every day that passed meant people would get bigger and smarter in their hostility. Staying put was a bullseye. We had to be on the move or be prepared to defend against takeover.

My mother might have joined me if not for my father. His aging body had failed him decades ago and he could hardly march a mile let alone the persistent trek we're expecting. My brother and sister and their spouses argued. It'd been tense for weeks anyway. This was just what they needed to let it all out. Sister cried. Brother argued in his way, so self-assured of his opinion that everything would work out. Deluded to the point that, despite having abandoned his own home, he was certain my house in which they bunkered would survive the onslaught. Denial, most definitely, but we didn't have time to wait for him to come around.

They all helped me and the kids pack and we said our goodbyes, treating it like a farewell before a long vacation rather than what it really was.

We split at dawn. My eldest sobbed. My youngest was uncharacteristically quiet. We spent the night in the dirt at top of Apache Mountain, a trail I used to hike back in the regular days.

It was there, in the dirt, in the dark and quiet and cold, holding my weeping children to my chest, that the first fire erupted. The flames ignited frighteningly close to our home. I couldn't be sure from the distance whether it was our neighborhood or not, but I hoped it wasn't. Or maybe I hoped it was because that would mean I was right to leave. Fleeing wasn't rash nor was it suicide, it was survival. I wanted to call home but wouldn't dare. If the family was hiding the noise would only cause them more issues. Perhaps even kill them. That was if their phones even worked. Reception was spotty of late, and electricity flickered off and on at random hours. Soon, these fucking phones wouldn't be worth more than the plastic they were made of anyway.

I didn't explain the fires to my kids, and they didn't ask about them. The sight of them stopped my eldest's crying, though.

~The Woman

MAYBE FEBRUARY SOMETHING? 2025

I haven't written in a while. I don't know what to say. Eldest got an ear infection. Took us a week to find antibiotics. He was in so much pain that he vomited three times. I vomited later as well, once he was out of earshot, as panic consumed all my senses. The idea of burying a child is always on the brain when you're a parent. The gloom of it shadows every happy moment of your life. But this was something else—I was screaming for help and looking for shovels. It was visceral. If not for my other child I would have dug a hole for two, but then we found Cheeks. He won't tell us his real name. Says he keeps his secrets in his cheeks, hence the name. He had penicillin. His roommate's prescription. Said they ran out the house and didn't need it. I'm sure it was stolen, as if I gave a shit. We traded water for three pills. Thankfully, it was enough. Eldest is recovering, although he doesn't hear as well out of his left ear anymore. A small inconvenience well worth his survival.

It's all I can do but think of my husband. We used to joke about the type of feral apocalypse people we would be, how well we would mesh under this very particular brand of stress. I don't know why we did this, but the banter felt reassuring in a way. But he died and now I'm out here alone. I try not to cry for him, but I do every night after the kids fall asleep. That motherfucker left me here by myself and I don't know what to do.

The kids cling to my side as if glued there, which I prefer. I have waking nightmares every night in which they are missing, stolen away in the night. Sometimes I see drag marks in the dirt or torn shreds of their clothing. I wake up over and over again, repeating the misery, until reality finally snatches me awake. Their warm bodies are all that keep me functioning at a reasonable level. Otherwise, I'd have traded my body for drugs long ago and OD'd under an overpass.

We are orbiting the downtown area lately, sleeping under trees and hiding behind bushes. It's a deadly choice, every night risks ambush and attack, but roaming is the only way to keep your eyes on the horizon. The desert fucking sucks, and water is scarce now that the municipal water supply has been contaminated by neglect, but the communities with water are impossible to infiltrate and even harder to maintain. They dissolve within months due to infighting and mismanagement. We trade when we can, but that too is dangerous.

Cheeks decided to travel with us. He was incredibly lonely. I get the sense that he roamed the streets even in the comfortable times, but he doesn't say much. It's nice to have another adult around to keep watch, a man to buffer the children against the violence slowly weaving its way into their DNA. The way he looks at my boys tears my heart in two. He has lost someone. He mourns them every time my children speak.

There has been no word from home. I didn't expect it, as much as I'd hoped for it. Phones no longer function except in rare cases. To find my family I would have to return to the rubble of our home, and I refuse to let me boys see that. I can only pray for them, whatever good it will do, and hope we stumble upon each other again.

I hope they are out there wandering. I hope they made it out. And if they didn't, I hope I find the fuckers that killed them so I can rip their throats out with my teeth.

~The Woman

PROBABLY FEB STILL, I DUNNO

I don't even know why I write anymore. These letters are a weight I don't need. They do not soothe, only enrage. We have been on our feet and moving for weeks. We are tired and dirty. We are thirsty most of the time. Youngest collapsed the other day from exhaustion or dehydration or both. We had to hide and pray we weren't found. Cheeks left to find water and came back with an unopened bottle of Gatorade. I have no idea how he managed to steal it, and he wouldn't say.

It is quite astounding how quickly we mutated as a society. So much of the decline happened in the shadows that mayhem landed at our feet seemingly overnight. I can still see my father's face when we told him we were leaving. The pain, pure and complete desperation to keep us, to have this world not swallow us whole, it was the most palpable emotion I have ever seen on another human. He was furious. He threatened to take my children from me.

And then we watched the fire consume our home from the mountain. How quickly our decision went from rash to in-the-nick-of-time. A coin flip the other way and all of us might be dead.

The cities are not the dystopian cage fights I make them out to be either. The mask of civility still holds strong in many places—usually the ones with fire power. But little infant authoritarian regimes are rapidly growing, becoming unruly teenagers, and then duking it out in the streets. For every 10 days of "normalcy" there are 30 minutes of death that may or may not find its way to your doorstep. We choose to avoid this risk, trading shelter, food, and stability for the obscurity of the fringes. Some kids still get to go to school. Eldest hated school, but the other day he sobbed, wishing to go back. I don't have the heart to tell him that his school doesn't exist anymore, even if the bricks that made it are still standing.

Personally, algebra is not worth the risk anymore, and so I keep my children with me, even if they'll hate me for it later.

Then again, not all is horrible. Another perplexing facet of humanity is our propensity for wonder. On the siren days we always take shelter. The siren is more of a collective yelp, like coyotes, traveling in a wave from drifter to drifter as a warning to upcoming danger, and yet my little straggler group rejoices at the sound. It means we stop moving and rest. Eldest and Youngest have come up with a game of it—passersby are often rather ridiculous about the siren, especially those still accustomed to city life. They flail for cover. It is also when the dogs and cats begin to roam, what with all the stupid humans in hiding. Anyone who wanders past is given a name and a backstory. The other day, maybe a week ago? Who can tell anymore? One person was rushing because he was a serial pants pooper. Another was looking for boogers in the trash cans before hiding. They giggled in their new, silent way, and even if I couldn't hear it, I felt it. Joy has a way of doing that, being felt like the heat from a torch.

They also like the dogs, whenever one of them dares to get close.

We find way to make it tolerable. This disaster must be tolerable. It must. Why else would we bother?

~The Woman

MARCH 2025

It's a toothache. A toothache. I know what the problem is. Cheeks knows it too. Youngest always had bad teeth—got them from his dad. So many cavities even though he brushed twice a day. Whatever ails him now probably began before the world fell apart. Now it is critical.

He has an infection. Abscess likely. His entire right cheek is red and swollen and hot to the touch. He will die without intervention. Cheeks told me about a friend on the streets who died of a toothache. It looked the very same, he said. The very same. Cheeks told me that he used to pull teeth from his mouth with pliers once they began to ache, then gargled his pain into oblivion with whiskey. Once his friend died, he stopped taking any chances. He's missing five teeth already.

But this is too far beyond a pair of pliers. Youngest needs a dentist. He needs medication, or else he is going to die.

Reality set in as soon as I saw the redness. Cheeks refuses to look me in the eye. My son will die, or else we will have to find something to trade for treatment, and there's nothing to trade besides what's between my legs.

I knew it would happen. I knew I would be forced to make this decision somehow. I have too many people with whom I am too invested in keeping alive. I try not to think about it as we head towards town.

It is what it is. This is the new world. Or maybe it's the old world circling back. This is how nothing has ever changed. The same of story, same sacrifice, same challenges, same pain. What a waste of progress. Look where we ended up?

~The Woman

I killed that piece of shit.
Youngest is recovering.
No one is speaking.
But I killed that piece of shit and it's over with.

TWO

A mother places her child on his knees, the barrel end of her pistol aiming at his tender scalp. She asks if he is sure but pulls the trigger before he can respond. Viscera sprays in red mist from the shot, this small explosion of death merely the precursor to what is coming—the bomb her son sent is only minutes from their heads.

The furious whine of panicked jets masks her maternal wail, a growl so potent her skin shivers with escape. Her son is dead in her arms, a seeping maw where his beautiful brown eyes should be, flesh sagging in place of his pink, chapped lips. Her boy, now a young man, but always her boy, who she has killed. He's sent the bomb, but he's sent it for her. She has never in her life been so astonished by betrayal.

The clouds float cautiously in the morning sky, jaundiced by a new-waking sun. This is good. She wouldn't see it coming as she scoops her son's lanky form into her arms, wouldn't see it as she shuffles forward, further from town, as if the bomb already set its sights on her back, as if it follows her and not the instructed coordinates set by her child. The jets above are loud now, louder than before. They are tracking the missile, guiding it toward her head. Any minute now. Any second.

The mother falls, curling around her son to preserve what of him remains unblemished, and then clutches him close, his body still pulsing warmth, still confused by its sudden, purgatorial existence straddling life and death. She doesn't even notice when the bombs hit—doesn't feel the blast of heat that peels her skin from her bones like scorched paper in a fire, particles of her blowing buckshot into the earth beneath her, a nuclear shadow of a mother cradling her son.

A radiated Pietà is all that that anyone will remember of them.

DATE 100? 1000?

They found us. I can't believe it, but they did. Old friends, coworkers. Scott heard about my little kerfuffle somehow. The story took on a life of its own, growing legs and hitting the streets. I thought I'd made a mistake allowing my name to get out. Perhaps not.

Scott had a few of his runners track us down. He's also high as kite every day, but that's beside the point. They found us in the desert, starved. I'd been too afraid to go back to the city. I didn't want to risk it.

Scott has a duplex. He gave us a bed. He fed the kids. They had potato chips. Scott even scrounged up some pop tarts for my youngest, remembering they were his favorite.

I sobbed into his arms. The kindness was unbearable.

Then we talked. He dipped in and out after stabbing his arm with something the color of danger, but Cheeks and I all had a few beers and talked until out voices cracked. We hadn't spoken this much in months. The kids fell fast asleep. Youngest snored like he used to when he was a baby.

In between nods, Scott told me that his brother and niece were missing. His parents were dead, having been stabbed during some infighting. He hadn't had any word on my family, but when he heard the story of the dentist, he said he knew it had been me. Gut told him. Or maybe he willed it into being, he said. Said he wanted it to be someone he knew so badly that it became so. I said that our paths twisted together so many times before, it only made sense for it to happen again.

I don't know why he thought it was me, honestly. There are so many 'me's' now. Same name, same face, but he said he just knew. I think he is just speaking out of his high ass.

Still, I love him dearly. Seeing him broke me for a million reasons. Look at this world, this fucking world. Why do we keep bothering to live it?

I say that shit and then I hear my kids' voices. I know why we live it. I live it for them. Parenting makes you miserable. It's a curse you'd never give away. A curse you take on your shoulders and heft into the sun. It makes everything before inconsequential so that your brain doesn't even bother to hold onto anything else. Life is split in two—before kids and after kids. Before kids could mean I was a toddler or an adult. It's a massive swath of time, and yet that statement, before kids is always enough. Before kids is all it takes to impart information, at least it is to the other cursed. Before kids means 'back when my life didn't amount to shit'.

But living means something now. It has purpose, even if I hate it. I'll never hate my kids, but I do hate the curse. I would love to slip beneath the veil like Scott and disappear, but I can't. I have to stay in the daylight, sun ripping flesh from bone to keep my progeny alive. I feel us changing. All of us are changing.

A piece of me died when I had kids, and another died when I yanked them from their beds and into the desert.

I missed Scott, and I hate him too. He reminds me of too much. For that I'll cherish him until I die. God help us.

~The Woman

MAY, LAST I HEARD, 2025

We might have stayed here too long. I keep trying to dismiss the idea, but the itch to run won't go away. I wish I had someone else to talk to about it, someone who loves my kids like I do. Sometimes I pretend their dad is still alive and I talk to him like he's simply on the other end of a blue tooth an not dead. I try to think about what he would say, if he would agree that we were getting too comfortable. He was always the more cautious of the two of us, which doesn't help my unease because in my gut I know what he'd recommend. At night when I'm alone I argue with him. I just can't imagine ripping my kids away from the only stability they've known since shit fell apart.

Cheeks is quiet. He used to be my ally but now he's getting comfortable here in needle kingdom. High all the damn time. Everyone is spiraling. Comfort in this life never lasts. You either watch it implode around you or die in the dream. It will not last. The kids are not safe here anymore. None of us are.

Scott is explosive. Loud. He yells until the walls shake. Never at us, but the kids run behind me every time. Cheeks continually insists these implosions are still better than the wilds. The infection, the starvation, the unknown. Here our beasts ring the fucking doorbell. Is that really any better?

One night when I was drunk I told Scott I would kill him if he ever hurt my kids. He got a look on his face that was enough to undo me—pained beyond imagining. How am I this person to everyone I know? I feel like everything and everyone is changing, and me too, but at a different speed. Like I'm already decades ahead and I'm just furious that they refuse to catch up. Cheeks calls it a symptom of my arrogance. True, surely. But that's how shit gets done and these soft-bellied men surrounding me are useless.

Scott keeps a stash of guns in the basement. He has no idea how many guns I've stolen, hidden around the house. He's too high to show me how to work them all, but I make a point to shoot them when the crew gets too fucked up. So high they can't apply the pressure to the trigger.

It would be so easy, you know.

~The Woman

SUMMER(ISH), 2025

Youngest found a glock (leave it it to Youngest to sow disorder). He brought it to Scott before I could stop him. Scott lost his mind. He was about to beat the shit out of Aaron G, the one in charge of the weapons closet, before I fessed up. I admitted to stashing guns because I was scared, and because they were wasted all the time. I returned all of them besides two.

I knew they'd go looking. Couldn't keep it quiet anymore. I gave them up but the best hidden. Those were the ones no one would miss anyway. The ones they wouldn't think of when doing a count.

A .22 is still better than nothing though. Scott pinned me to the wall by my neck. Eldest flipped. Scott apologized. Youngest cried.

I knew we should have left by now, and if my husband was here I know he'd say this was all my fault and he'd be right. Had I not taken anything none of this would have happened. At least not now. It would have eventually. How could it not? Drugs and guns and lawlessness and foolishness always equals violence.

I know if I step out of line again they might kill me. If I leave, they will track me down because I will have taken more than a few things with me on my way out. That night, Eldest cried into my chest. He asked if we were going back to the desert.

So we won't leave. And when I get caught again it will only be because I was ready. God Jesus almighty, I hope I am ready.

I spoke to Aaron F (there are two of them, go figure) after the fallout. He said he found 3 of the guns I'd taken. He also said he knew it was me. He caught me once, but never said a word.

He is the only sober one of the crew anymore. Us showing up that day, he says, was an act of God. I laughed in his face. All the former program junkies spew on and on about God. It's boring. I used to not care, but I do now. So fucking boring. There is no God for us. There is no meaning. It's freeing in a way, to think of being alone. Truly alone. On a rock spinning in the dark with other ants. What do Gods have to do with it? What does morality have to do with anything? Who does goodness serve anymore? Not me, that's for fucking sure.

Aaron F doesn't bristle when I spit on his beliefs. Somehow, it must all tie into what he has decided about me and my family. He and Cheeks smoke cigarettes on the patio and play cards a lot.

So we stay. We stay because it's what we have to do to stay whole. It's funny how that is literally the only thing that matters anymore. Another freedom, I guess, to have one's priorities whittled away until only one remains.

I better be ready for when Scott catches wise to my tricks, that is if he doesn't strangle me to death first. I don't think he *wants* to kill people, but that's never stopped him before.

~The Woman

DATE OF A NEW DAY

I don't know what happened. I don't. I don't know how. Everything is in pieces.

Lol just kidding. I know exactly how it happened. L.O.L. I haven't said that in a beat. LOL. Lolololololololol.

Fucking high morons.

It was my talk with Aaron F that sealed it. Animals on a rock. Civility is for the fucking rich. Let the president be civil. He can practice civility while I make my way to his door drenched in blood.

Scott, well, he didn't make it. I tried to explain that he was spiraling. He was too high all the time to manage the little corner store empire he created. The vultures were circling, they were gonna claim him and everything he owns. Us. My kids. Sell us for parts.

I don't give a fuck if it was mine to take, because I took it anyway. He said he'd kill me.

He didn't.

His loyal few are dead too. Couldn't be risked. Some of them I liked, but most were nothing but waste. Half dead vessels. They're better off, or that might just be what I tell myself.

The vultures will hear of it. They will come for inspection, and I'll give them everything they want. They and I have different sights.

Aaron F, or just Aaron now, won't make eye contact anymore. Fucking men, so ineffectual, and yet still able to make me doubt myself. My husband would hate me for what I've done. My kids, of course, don't understand the implications of our new status, and no one would dare tell them. I don't want them to hate me, I really don't. I don't want them to be afraid of me, but someone had to act and I'm the only mother they have.

If the kids find out and they do hate me, hopefully they'll come to understand the gift it is to be alive to do so.

~The Woman

Things to do:

1. *Eat*
2. *Get water*
3. *Control water*
4. *Electricity flickering. Stop the flickering.*
5. *Kids*
6. *Send someone after Cheeks*
7. *Make list*
8. *Stick to list*
9. *This list is bullshit*
10. *It's all bullshit*
11. *Bullshit*
12. *Bull*
13. *Shit*

SUMMER? STILL BLAZING HOT, BUT THAT DOESN'T MEAN MUCH HERE, 2025

There comes a time for every parent where you look at your child and think, just, what the fuck?

What the fuck is this about? What biological urge drives me to be this way, to act this way? The irresistible obsession a mother has with their children. It isn't biological in the sense that it arrives with birth. Anyone can become a mother to a child. But a moment comes in the relationship when something snaps—breaks you like hollow bird bone, and all that keeps you whole is that child. That's it.

We sat around the fire last night. Only then, in the shifting shadows and lights did I catch my children's growth. Half a year, at least, has passed. Eldest has a granite chin like his dad. Youngest smirks all the time, his lips sucked into his teeth. That night neither said a word, just glared as if hypnotized into the flames. And I was hypnotized by them. Mesmerized. It was just the three of us, and I thought then, so crystal clear and vivid as a splinter in the skin, that they were it. I have been falling and falling. Doing things for the sake of keeping busy. Imparting authority but to the wrong people. We have a crew now, thirty strong, and to be so busy now, so many issues and mouths and strains and needs kept my suicidal brain occupied. But why do it?

For my kids, obviously. Any mother would say the same. We do it for them. It makes all life's transgressions against us sting less, even though they cut deeper.

Power. Wealth. Dominance. All these are distractions. They mean less than the paper I write this on. They might do damage, but they mean nothing. They are substitutes for what really matters.

And, God, are so many people so fucking stupid. Most just can't see through the fog. And because of this they stand no chance of stopping me.

~The Woman

A NEW YEAR. DAY ONE. JANUARY 2026

It's been a while.

A lot has happened. A lot. I'm not even sure where to begin, or even why I'm bothering. Or, I guess I know, but it pains me to admit it. So, I won't.

We took control of the water in Saguaro County. It's a small county, not the main metro area which still has some government oversight. The team is still small, but we have collected enough recruits to appear more imposing than we are. I suppose I shouldn't say such things should anyone find this, but I am bored so I don't care.

There isn't much to SawCo (short for Saguaro County, which sounds like Sah-wor-roh, which means writing SagCo looks weird because my brain immediately wants to read it as Sag-Co, but I digress) besides trailer parks and a somehow functioning 24 hour liquor store, but to them, I am a God. And that is the point. To the facility employees, I am nothing more than small time mob boss, looking for a cut. I don't have eyes on the inside yet, but I will before long. Until then, I just need to prove that I will keep my word, until such a time I can force the issue. I'm sure some of them are thinking the same thing, but I'm not worried. I have their families at my fingertips. By the time they dare, it will be too late.

We treat them well, guarantee them water and protection, and they protect our borders with ferocity. Nothing is a more effective deterrent than a band of crazed hillbillies with nothing but boredom to protect, so it keeps even the nosiest wanderers away, which is what we need right now.

Things are still fluid. Aaron's engineering inclinations have been put to serious use. He alone has rigged every square inch of our home with cameras and explosives, which occasionally blow-up prairie dogs and rats.

The kids are thriving more than I could have ever hoped. Thriving after watching their home burn from atop the mountain, knowing that the only surviving family was sitting next to them. While missing school and starving and nearly dying from some fucking virus that brought eldest to his knees. They are thriving. They smile. They laugh. They can shoot a gun and skin a rabbit. They play games again. And at night, they sleep. I know this because they tell me when they can't.

Sometimes, in the dark, I still think of my husband. He would hate my guts for what I've become.

~The Woman

FEBRUARY 13TH, 2026 (THE WATER PLANT KEEPS AN ACCURATE DATE)

There was a revolt at the water treatment center. Whichever idiot in charge decided to blackmail one of my guys. It was stupid too, not even for much money. I was tempted to give it to him, let him think for just a bit longer that he was in charge, but it was Aaron, of all people, who talked me out of it. That was as far as he was willing to go, though. The follow through was left for me. So I found this guy's kid. Not sure how many he has, because he was slightly clever enough to spread his family around the town, stuffing each into a different home hoping we wouldn't sniff them out. This teenager, Paul, was the one to find this kid—who we originally assumed was his nephew. Frankly, nephews are just as valuable during these after times. Any family is valuable, so I wasn't terribly concerned one way or another. The kid was young enough that harm to him would hopefully be intolerable.

So 'Idiot A' shows up to the door, the meeting place. Says he wants another hundred per week or he'll shut the facility down. I tell him that if he wants to kill the town to be my guest, but that this kid I found will be the first to die, right then and there. Kid is terrified, doesn't know I'm not going to hurt him. The look on Idiot A's face, the terror, I know it intimately. I feel it when I look at my own kids. This is no nephew. This is a son. Probably ten years old by the looks of him, too.

No no, he says. I can work for the same wage. I'm just trying to provide for my family. Yada yada, as if I'm stupid. I say I understand. That's all any of us are trying to do. It's just that some of us are better than others, and I have no use for morons.

We send the kid away. Idiot is shot. This problem is solved, but the solution creates another.

We take the facility and we tell them the truth. Idiot tried to get wise. He's dead now. You can work for us and keep this place going, or we can kill you too and do our best without you. And if we fuck that up, all your families die from dehydration and god knows what else. What say you?

But we all know what they said. They said the same thing any frightened yet reasonable person would say—Yes sir. Yes ma'am. Whatever you want.

What you must watch for is the moment fear gives way to monotony. That's when another crop of idiots rises. Hopefully they too will listen to the reason presented to them.

~The Woman

THREE

A mother sits with her youngest son, backs leaning against the abandoned posts which used to uphold a security fence. Their home is quiet. The people have fled.

They pass a blunt between them, alternating ferocious coughs because neither could ever get the hang of smoking. Their lungs rebuke it, the process of inhaling suddenly fraught with disaster. But they need to get high and stay high today. There is no other way.

The son recovers, pinching poison between his delicate fingers. The mother winces at the sight of her child's drawn features, how the blunt trembles in his grip, and how he bites his lower lip like he did as a toddler when getting scolded. Part of her wishes she'd not warned the town, forcing everyone to dissolve into ash. All of them are fucked anyway. Sure, they can run far away, but they are not quick enough. The mother knows this. So does the son. Now their last moments are spent wallowing in terror instead of doing whatever the fuck else they might be doing. She steals the blunt back. Very soon, none of this will matter because she will be dead.

"Do you feel it?" she asks. Her son has taken plenty of shallow drags but nothing substantial. He's nervous, scared, and smoking weed with his mother for the first time.

He shakes his head with enough disjointed clumsiness to know he's lying. Good. That's good—numb up, baby boy.

Somewhere in the distance, jets are circling.

"What about Eldest?" the son asks. "How far away do you think he got?"

The mother doesn't even want to think about her other son, so she shrugs, imagining him gazing down upon them like a god or a damaged child trying to rouse a dead goldfish in the bowl, tears streaming, screaming *wake up wake up* all while knowing the fish is dead because he's too intelligent not to know that the fish is dead. The mother hopes he is out there, looming in a shadowy corner because that means he might live.

She does not know where he is, though. And now she never will.

"What happened to Jennie?" the boy asks.

The mother snuffs the blunt into the dirt. That's quite enough of that.

"How honest do you want our last moments to be?" she says.

Sometimes she forgets which of her kids she is speaking to. Eldest would understand the deflection immediately. In that way, it is much easier to talk to him. He understands her. He knows who she is. This is also why he left.

But Youngest always needs her to articulate. Innuendo never lands right. Nuance bypasses him completely. If he asks a question, he wants a straight answer.

"Who cares?" he says.

The mother figures this is the final thing she can do for the son she has ruined, so, leaning her head onto his shoulder, she thinks to say, "I choked her."

But the words never form, instead scattering amongst the vicious rush of radiated light.

MARCH 1ST, 2026

What do I do with all this bottled rage? Who do I give it to? Because I can't keep it. I seethe constantly. My new perma-state is incandescence. Simple tasks take twice as long because I need to orient myself. I stare at the wall, grind my teeth to nubs, coating all directive with enamel powder. What am I supposed to do with this?

Sex helps, but only briefly, and only if they're good. Otherwise, I am so much worse. Angry at their silly bodies and the withering thing I call my own. What am I supposed to do with it besides bottle it up, compress it, release it only when useful. A nuclear device in my chest. It will detonate eventually. Something this potent never settles. I cannot settle. I cannot function.

The kids. The kids are all there are to spur a lull. To stroke their cheeks is to trigger hibernation, to be possessed by a future where I fail them, which terrifies me. Their voices are a balm, the only one.

God help me if I fail them. If I can't protect them. What if I'm the one that ruins them? What if I already have?

I am often asked if I miss the old life, and when I think of it, of our home, of the simple things that used to well a fury so white hot I dreamed of slitting throats over a dirty pair of underwear, I always say no. And it's true. I don't miss the before, and I don't long for it. And when others agree, those who say they don't miss the before because the memory is too painful, because they won't ever be able to wake up again and face a new day—to those I nod my head and agree. Yes, that's it, I say. Too difficult.

But that isn't it. I just don't miss it.

I don't miss it, but I sure wish I knew what to do with all this bottle rage.

Pressurized piece of shit.

~The Woman

MARCH 15TH, 2026

Nothing makes me happy anymore. Happiness shouldn't matter—it factors into nothing these days. But the crushing weight of apathy grinds a person down. It feels like walking in water, everything is distorted, decision making slows as I try to make sense of my surroundings. I take a few beats too long to make decisions, and even then, I'm not sure if they are good. And I don't really care if they are good decisions, because if it ruins me then I don't have to worry about anything anymore. This is depression, probably. But who cares? Who isn't fucking depressed? Part of me is depressed because everyone else is, and maybe they're depressed because of me. A big old circle of fucking lunatics.

Who do you talk to when no one is right? I guess I talk to yourself, or the amorphous reader of these letters. I speak to you, so you understand. Humans are too luxurious. Or at least my generation is. The in-betweens. The people with one foot in either life. It is impossible to reconcile and impossible to live. We survive, but we are already destroyed.

We will make the next set a little stronger, a little more resilient. They will know nothing else, so joy will come to them in whichever ways they invent. Our invented ways are dead, and therefore so are we.

We just need to live a little longer to get these babies grown. After that, we bow out and leave, crossing our fingers and wishing them luck like a swamp hag might spit a curse.

Don't fuck it up, you little shits.

~The Woman

APRIL 22ND, 2026

Eldest got into a fight today. The last creature on this earth I would expect to do so. He was a little mirror of his mother, or that's what everyone that saw it said.

Look at him! An awed sort of compliment, as if his despair was a good thing. It was, I guess. I needed to see his teeth, if only once, just to know he could feed himself if I die tomorrow. But it also scared me.

Aaron said it's normal for his age. Which, yeah, probably. Maybe some of it. But I know this boy, this sweet baby of mine. The baby that never liked to be held but always needed reassurance. The baby that loved trains and would wear his conductor hat to bed. The baby that had his first anxiety attack when we took away his pacifier at 3 years old, so fierce that I'm not sure he ever recovered, as if that simply act of ripping the comfort from his mouth ruined his little psyche for good, an imprint on it until it bubbled over to today. I don't even know what the fight was about— I just saw him choking on the elbow of some random townie. Not sure the dude even knew who Eldest was, but he figured it out quick when Aaron rolled up to his defense, then me shortly after. Didn't do anything to them but break them up, but Eldest was spitting mad, and the townie damn near choked on his apologies. Eldest refused to come out of his room afterwards. I think I embarrassed him. Probably not wise, but shit, he is still my kid.

Aaron says he will talk to Eldest, and I suppose he should, man to man, someone who understands the surge of testosterone that comes with puberty.

I would kill to feel so fucking alive like that, I have to keep my rage in a jar and use sparingly because it spoils to suicide when exposed too long to air. What am I even talking about? I really think I sound clever, don't I?

Fuck, but Eldest, that sweet boy, something in him went dark today. Maybe it was the boy in him. Youngest clings to my legs more and more lately. Will his little light dim too one day?

When it does, I guess that means the old life will have truly and finally died. Perhaps then I can bury it for good.

~The Woman

SUMMER (I'M FUCKING WASTED), 2026

Aaron asked about children. About what it was like to love your children. To raise them. To care for them. I've been thinking about this a lot lately, especially as my life is squeezed into tight focus, the ancillary shit sloughing away into memory.

Love is an empty word. It's too vague. Insufficient. What does it mean to love? How can one love a partner and love a parent and also love a child? How can those all be described with the same word?

I think love is about needing someone, and them needing you back. With a partner you need their affection, their touch, their sex. With a parent, you need their comfort and protection. Their safety.

Your needs as a parent, your needs for your kids, are where things get hairy. The love of a child is the only kind described with needs you can't possibly fulfill. As a parent, you need your child to live. You need them to thrive, to be happy, you need them to make smart choices, you need them to smile. How do you give another human a smile? How to make them thrive? You need to do these things because these little humans become your sun. They need to thrive because if they don't, you both wither on the vine. Parents try to provide the things they need from their kids with money, whichever luxuries they believe will deliver happiness, but our zeal to fulfill this need doesn't always promote the best choices.

Love for children is the most desperate act on the planet because it is so unattainable. A touch from a partner can fill such a void, but a frown from your child and tear your soul to irreparable shreds.

All this to say it's just different. Everyone always said so, but to articulate it is something else.

I said all this and then I told him about youngest's eyes. In the before time, we had a fire pit in the backyard. I'd taken a couple edibles and their dad lit the fire and the four of us squished onto the patio furniture only made for three. Youngest crammed next to me, partially on my lap, his spindly nine-year-old legs folded into his chest, and he just talked. Very unlike now, the kid used to ramble and ramble about the weirdest shit, some video game I didn't understand, asking what rocks were made of, reciting his numbers one through ten in twenty different languages just because he could. He spoke without a captive audience, he never needed one, class participation was irrelevant, and usually I would nod robotically, repeat a word or two back to him and say "oh yeah?". This was usually enough for him and for me. I didn't understand a damn word he said anyway.

But that night, high off my ass, this kid literally alight from the flames in front of us, he was so happy. In that moment he was thriving. In that little sliver of night, he was fulfilled. And I thought, fuck, if I could cut this moment free from the stream and just live in it forever, I would. I say this very seriously, but the meaning of life was there in his eyes that night.

And then the dog, confused by the reflection of the fire pit, jumped into the closed glass door thinking it was open. The thump of his stupid little head dissolved everything, and the moment was gone. I don't know if I ever found it again, or if I did I was too dumb to see it.

I told Aaron all this and the way he stared back at me felt strange. He said my explanation made more sense to him than any other, and I felt good about that. My love for words has faltered of late, I say less and less, except here. I miss it. I'm best with my words. It felt very good to know something of mine reached another, something other than my anger.

We fucked after that, something we've done often enough, but he didn't leave afterward like he usually did.

I didn't mind, either.

~The Woman

DATE WHATEVER

Do you know what it is like to write under the constant strain of destruction? I wonder if you do. Though I loathe the word creativity, it is the only suitable choice for what I mean. Creativity is a luxury, or should I say, artistic creativity is a luxury. One must be creative to survive pandemics and wars and the constant threat of annihilation. Creativity is what keeps you alive.

But art? Art is for the privileged. Everything about it screams "I have time to waste."

Time to waste? What a luxury. How beautifully luxurious. I suppose I steal moments for this journal or whatever I am calling it, and that is a privilege I have that others do not, but I no longer give a fuck about checking my privilege. What a stupid fucking word. What a goddamn crock of shit. We used to have time to yell about such things, to try and ruin people's lives and careers and reputations over things like misused, misappropriated, and misguided privilege. What a time to be alive!

Maybe it's the cynic in me but it satisfies me to think that very few of those pearl-clutchers survived. All your online posturing got you was an early grave, you useless infant. A lot more of you should have dug trenches for a living. You might still be breathing today, instead rotting underground, your bachelor's degree fertilizing my food. I mean, good for you, I guess. I never got my degree.

I think though, I think I'm just so angry. I'm so murderously furious that everyone is an enemy. Some of those I revile really did try—they tried to do good, tried to be good. But still, they're dead. They are dead. They don't make art anymore. They don't fuss over plot holes or worldbuilding. That shit is for the rich. That was their privilege and the people in charge crushed them to dust. Then I come along to sweep up the remains, tossing them into the dustpan on my hip, picking out the goods and scattering the rest on radiated wind.

Aaron says I think too much about this kind of shit. He says I am too much in my head. My husband used to say that too, back in the before times, before his illness, when we would fight about the stupidest shit. Can you believe we used to fight about sex? I can't believe it either. How fucking asinine. To think that I held my body with such regard, a temple, my palace, whatever the hell I thought. It was mine, and I was clinging to it like a dying monarch. My words—mine. My thoughts—mine. My body—MINE. And I was not willing to share. Nor did I have to—no one is owed any of those things. Even now, I choose who and how, but back then I kept myself sacred on purpose. As a weapon. Because my husband was lazy and annoying. Frankly, I did not like him at all when he was alive. Divorce is what we should have done, but neither of us had the courage. Instead, I withdrew deeper into my palace and barred the gates. Electrified that shit. To touch me was to know pain. And I thought that this would get through to him that I wanted him out, all while hanging a little welcome sign on the door to danger because I was too chickenshit to just come out with it. To just say fuck you, I can't stand this, let's be done. And he was too frightened to acknowledge that he knew I wanted to leave. So we both orbited each other, flinging venom at each other, both confident that the other was the villain of the story.

But sex is still sex. The animal pleasure of it heals so much. Fuck, we might have tolerated each other a bit better had I just realized that a little sooner. My husband might not be the weird recluse he became before he died, lingering like a gnat on the fringe just for the opportunity to glimpse one of his kids. Our toxic tête-à-tête eventually ruined him. I ruined him.

But Aaron says I think too much about this old world stuff. I know he is right, but how can I not when its ghost bores weepy contempt into my back wherever I go? How can I not meander back and puzzle out how a person I once loved died hating me as much as I hated him?

Aaron says a lot of shit he shouldn't.

~The Woman

AUGUST (ALREADY?)

Time to move.
Time. To. Move.

SawCo moving outward and upward. We've grown too large. Don't have enough space. Too many people, too much infighting. We are bored and lawless. People need law, and fear, and war, something to conquer in order to keep them quiet. If we succeed, great, but if we fail, we've thinned the herd enough to keep food on the plates of the survivors.

And we just might succeed. It's an easy take, considering the surprising and sudden might of our little army. We have many restless souls. Some dirty siren called them here. Friend of a friend. Word of mouth still means the most, even now. Something our digital past never grasped. Everything dissolves against the weight of human breath, crumbles under the smacking sound of lips. Real people, real hands to hands, teeth to teeth, that's how armies are made.

That's how we have made one. And that's how we will take the little Podunk nothing just south of us. They aren't bothering anyone aside from having the audacity to exist too near to us. But this is how it goes. They will have the choice—be absorbed, pay their dues, and keep on keeping on like they have with minimal interference. Or fight, and let it get bloody.

Believe me though, if we lose, we will only return, but now with a point to prove.

I remember a story I heard in the before time of some vicious queen that exacted revenge on the people that murdered her king husband. She lied, said she would marry her husband's murderer to unite the kingdoms, but when the envoy arrived she buried them alive. When the next envoy arrived, she killed them too, but not before showing them the rotting corpses of their fellows. Then, to prove a point, she sent word to her enemies that she would cease aggression if each household sent her a bird. She took the birds, tied incendiaries to their feet and set them free, knowing they would return to their normal roost. She burnt their city to the fucking ground, and to be exact, she sent her forces to surround the city, murdering or enslaving anyone who dared try to flee.

I always liked her. Ruthless. No prisoners. An absolute fucking demon. Evil, no doubt. Monstrous. But when war comes, when famine and pestilence ride in on his heels, Death not far behind, it is only the monstrous that make empires.

I guess that bit of me has always been there, lurking and waiting. I don't mind the sound of screams as much as I thought I would. How quickly it bores a person. Maybe that's the signal that they aren't a person anymore.

Doesn't matter. I'm alive. They are not.

~The Woman

(undated)

I'm struck by a memory today. I have tried to ignore it, but it nags like a stench. I can't shake the smell, which puzzles me, and hate not understanding my own thoughts.

I remember Youngest. Back in the before, back when we had a 2400sqft house and a yard that looked like it was haunted due to neglect, a garage filled with so much shit I couldn't ever park in it, and fake hardwood floors that were just starting to chip, way back then I had an office. Five bedrooms for a family of four. Both kids had a room, both adults their own office. And I was miserable. Stupid fool. Miserable! I had a house and bedroom and an office and a lovely home full of lived-in shit, two relatively happy kids, adjusted in all the ways you hope they adjust, and I was miserable. Anyway.

In this office was an elliptical machine my aunt had given me. Unlike the treadmill, I actually used the elliptical. I liked hiking more, but the elliptical would do. But the kids, they loved it. Drawn to it like bears to honey. Like little mosquitoes flirting with buzzy light disaster. I'd open the door to that office, and I swear those kids would manifest at the sound of my ass hitting the chair and launch onto the fucking elliptical. They loved it, and I hated that they loved it. Youngest especially would drive me up the wall. Too much like his dad, that kid. Attention span of a gnat. Anyway, Youngest would slam into that machine at full speed, whipping the pedals faster than they ought to ever go. They were meant for old-boned mothers, not a wild and vital youth, and I would be at my desk counting the seconds before I couldn't stand it anymore, before I snapped at him to knock it off because I was trying to focus (on what? My writing? Fucking idiot). He'd get this shit-eating grin, he didn't care, and two minutes later as I'm just settled from the first interruption, headphones on, moody music rolling, that's just when, laugh out loud, that damn kid would be back it. The pedals would whine, the energy suddenly so kinetic and spazzy that even if I didn't see him from the corner of my eye, or hear the whir of those pedals, I would know he was there.

Each time my patience would wane a little more until just the peripheral dash of him down the hall would make me tense. He couldn't step foot in my office without me squawking at him to leave. But it never bothered him. He'd just smirk, say okay, and try his luck again in a few minutes. Kid was fucking nine or ten and no better than a goldfish lapping a tiny bowl. Go go go. Always had to go, even when he was sitting still it was because his mind was GOING.

It struck me today as I rounded on Youngest after breakfast, knowing that, like usual, he'd barely eaten, and his sunken eyes lolled like wrecking balls towards me, like they were in pain, as his thin little lips formerly full of mirth and mischief remained rod straight and grim, that I hadn't seen that little smirk since the days of that office. He hadn't smiled. Not once, in my memory at least. I am so accustomed to this kid existing in his strange, untethered reality that I didn't notice him slipping away from me. So, I suppose I am not confused as to why the memory was so potent, or why I am compelled to write about it. I get it. I do.

Maybe I am just living in it as hard as I can because I know now that it was the last time. That was it. There have been a lot of lasts and a lot of maybes and a lot of loss, and maybe because Youngest was always so assured, not as fragile in his emotions as Eldest, needed fewer hugs and fewer still assurances to his worth, that I just didn't notice when he needed me most. I kept him alive, a feat I considered (still do) of the highest order. But now I see the cost paid. The true sacrifice of survival.

It is a bitter invoice.

(undated)

I see their eyes everywhere. My children. All the eyes of all the people I have had a hand in killing come with a pair of round, brown eyes I would recognize anywhere. When Youngest could barely raise his face to meet me, even as I yelled, I knew then that he'd died. The old him. The young him. That him was gone, and I killed him. I killed all of them.

And who is to blame beside me? Who is to blame for this? What do I do now? I don't know. I feel like I need to do something. SOMETHING. Something.

What do you do when you've squashed it all beneath your feet? When you're so used to squashing little things and all that's left are the big, unsquashable things and you've got nothing left to pulverize? What does a person do with those feet and those fists? I feel something simmering. Once you start down this path there is no stopping. I wish I knew that before. I suppose a logical person could have assumed it, musing from their armchair, their office with an elliptical machine, they could have known in the incorporeal way a person knows unknowable things, but it's a much fiercer pull, a feral thing, that power. I wish I would have known then, as we marched in pussy hats, threw bricks at congress, that those with the real power didn't look at us with disdain, but actually did not look at us at all. And if they thought about us, maybe while they were taking a shit or buying helicopters for their yachts or whatever powerful people used to do, it was only to cursorily quip "over my dead body, peasant."

Because that's what we had to do to stop this. To stop a rolling boulder such as power, you have to stone it dead and kill it. There is no such thing as negotiating.

We should have gone feral, matched their energy. Killed their wives while at pilates, killed their security detail while they were fucking the wives, dragged their raggedy offspring from their middle school science class by their hair and held them ransom. Should have killed their grocer, their cook, their dentist, anyone who so much as emptied their fucking trash, so that anyone worth rocks would know to stay far away. And then, when they were finally ostracized, terrified, and alone, then we should have killed them too. And even if we couldn't, well, the damage would have been done enough. It would still have been a win.

But we didn't do that. We were snowed, avalanched under a code of righteousness that only applied to us.

And now my kids are dying and dead, gone to all but memories, even as they walk beside me, sleep in their beds in my room, snoring softly in the thick of night. They are gone too, and there is only me to blame.

Us.

FOUR

A mother sits at her desk, trying to assuage the churn in her gut. She muses about the word assuage—how *her* mom used to pronounce it *assage*, as in massage, and how profoundly this mother missed those moments with her own. Her mom is dead. She held out hope for many years, scanning crowds for her mom's familiar mop of dyed red hair, but a person must move on after a while. The mother knows that if her mom is still alive, she'd have found her daughter by now.

All this thought did little to soothe the mother, the grim face of a dead matriarch now haunting her drawn eyelids like an omen. After so many years, she's come to believe in the animal instincts of man, her own having saved her repeatedly. Her current internal turmoil detects something—the electrical current of an intruder, the hot breath of a lurking predator that her 'elevated' brain was too busy to recognize. But there is nothing here. She is confidently secure in her office, a space she designed to keep her isolated and, hopefully, safe. Whatever disturbance lingering heavy enough in the air for her senses to sniff out would have to be monumental, so the mother rises from her chair and exits.

The surrounding house is quiet. She listens for her son, a boy she used to call Youngest for all intents and purposes, yet now calls him Only. He should be at his computer, blossoming adulthood making it difficult for him to draw his knees into the regular fetal squat of his younger years. He should be wide-eyed with a screen reflecting onto the reddened whites of his eyes. But he is gone as well.

The mother calls to him, not quite expecting a response but hoping all the same. She calls many times until a squawk of terror echoes back to her, its source obscured by the shadowy crevasse of the hallway.

She suspects it is her child, lurching over his knees as if sick.

"Mom," he says. "Mom, I've done something. I've done it."

Her head tilts up, neck cracking from the strain. The ceiling gapes back.

"Where?" she asks while gently touching his shoulder.

He can only mutter one word—home.

And she knows what is coming, so she slaps him, regretting it instantly and yanking him to her breast.

"This is some Icarus shit," she says to her boy. "Only I've thrown you into the sun myself."

He cries and cries, sputtering apologies she doesn't deserve.

They die together clutching in the hallway of an empty house, every memory of their existence incinerated against the sound of the fading whine of jets.

TIFFANY MEURET

SEPTEMBER 19ᵀᴴ, 2026

Aaron was the one to bring it up. Programming. Said he could set Youngest up with the guy running the software for the water facility. What the fuck did we have to lose? So I sent Youngest there. Said he needed to learn something outside of the cracks in our living room walls. Needed to get out. He sobbed at my leg when I tried to leave. I never saw that coming.

After he vomited, I sat him down away from everyone. The entire facility saw him meltdown. Not great. I needed him to know that, as much as I didn't want to be that person. He had to know that he was a target. Had to wrap it up, keep it down, see me in the shadows with that shit. Not here.

He nodded. This kid always seems to understand, or seems to, when you explain stuff flat out. He nodded, and he went back in.

Aaron kept an eye on him. Told me he didn't lift his head even once from the screen, as if he'd melted into it. The engineer leaned back in his chair, and after about an hour of complete indignation at my pull of power, of him having to babysit my unstable child while we all pretended it was for the good of the whole when really it's for the good of my own peace of mind, he finally squinted at the screen, slapping Youngest's hands away from the keyboard while he inspected what the kid had done. Then he asked Youngest to explain it to him. Not because the engineer didn't understand, but because he wanted to make sure Youngest did. After that, he approached Aaron and said, "I'll have a seat for him tomorrow. Have him here by sun up."

When I asked Youngest how it went, he shrugged. When asked if he wanted to go back, he said he didn't know. So I sent him back, and I have barely seen him since. Every day I wander through the treatment facility to check on him, as a threat to everyone, even Youngest, that I am always watching, and Youngest rarely acknowledges me. I prefer it that way—I know he is focused on something other than his misery.

Eldest floated aimless for the first week or so, distraught without someone to care for every waking moment, but now seems to have adjusted nicely to his new freedom. He started talking to a few other kids his age, albeit awkwardly. Aaron worries, but he always worries. I must have a type. Perhaps I need that canary in the coal mine to keep me rational. That's probably it.

SEPTEMBER 24TH, 2026

That podunk town was easily sacked. The word sounds stupid. Sacked. It sounds antiquated. We used to sack cities, now we...what? Destroy? Occupy? Raze?

It wasn't so much a city as a small shanty village. A bunch of stragglers—displaced and scared and beaten and starving people. It was such a non-event that I didn't deign to mention it before now. It didn't even merit discussion, because once we rolled up, the people spewed free of their tents and practically bowed their noses to the dirt. There was no conflict there. Those that itched for blood, high on adrenaline and probably meth, they attacked each other. We lost a few. Those that went in too hard were shot on sight. Two by Aaron, one by me, and a few other offshoots that Aaron issued to his grunts, but not without his aw shucks, kick at the dirt hangdog expression. He does it because he knows he has too. Can't have that kind of rabid shit within the ranks. It poisons the well.

I do it because I am fucking furious, just, all the time.

But that isn't why I write about it now. The invasion, the sacking, whatever we call it, came up today. Eldest instigated, as he seems wont to do lately. He's so much like his dad. He asked if we were (are) the good guys. And he's young, but not so young as to not give him an answer. The good guys? They were never real, and they certainly don't exist here now. The good guys, by whatever metric he is using (defined by the before time), well, those dumb motherfuckers are dead. The good guys of before were too goddamn stupid to stay alive if not for being lifted atop the shoulders of worshippers. Useless sacks of meat. But how does a mother say such a thing to her child? A child who wants to be good. A child, whom this mother loves with every atom of her being, who still defines themselves by the act of goodness.

I didn't say anything. Probably not the best thing to do, but I was blindsided. I was ashamed, in a way, because I didn't have the stones to tell my kid that I no longer cared if I was a good guy. I used to. I prided myself on the fact that I was reasonable and good. A moderate. Because all the things that make a person "good" can also make a person "bad". Honesty without tact is cruelty, they say.

But take compassion, for one. Great in small doses. Reasonable doses, but people eventually showed us how useful compassion was. How dysfunctional compassion can be. There are atrocities everywhere. Every day. Crises every day. Torture every day. Seeing it all cripples the overtly compassionate. They can save no one, solve nothing, because the things they want to save and solve are so far removed from their reach they are almost impossible. They can be compassionate to their neighbor, to a homeless person on the street, but why bother when the world is already dying? They crumble, they become panicked by their uselessness, and they do nothing. Oh, they scolded online, no doubt about that, but then they went home, watched youtube, and consumed so many edibles they were still couch locked in the morning, which is what we all did and labeled it as self-care.

But I no longer bother with goodness. Goodness is for the powerless. Power is for the powerful. And power is all that matters here. It's all that ever mattered. Now to explain that to my kid. He will probably hate me once I do. I know he will. Which is why I stayed quiet.

OCTOBER 2026

I shit my pants today. I swear to God. I don't even think I'm sick. I was walking the perimeter as I tend to do when I'm restless, which is every day. Felt a little crampy but it faded. Then, it didn't. My stomach knotted up and I knew I was in trouble. Would have been funny too, if I was anyone but who I am. Shitting your pants is always funny. It's one of the commonalities of the before time and the now. Poop and farts will always be funny. You can count on it.

But anyway, I had to walkie Aaron. Couldn't tell him what happened in case anyone was listening. Can't let them know the boss is getting older and crapping her pants like an Alzheimer's patient. I told him to bring the truck and a couple of towels. So he rolls up. All panicked thinking I killed a guy or something, and I just hold my hand up like "I shit my pants, you gotta get me back without anyone knowing."

He didn't believe me. Stepped toward me as if to challenge me. Then he spotted my shoes. I didn't catch that the shit had leaked from the cuffs of my pants and onto my shoe. He lost his mind. Hurled a towel at me and called me gross. I told him I'd throw it at him like a fucking monkey and he laughed again. It felt good to make him laugh. I don't think I've heard much of that lately.

He drove me to the house in the back of his truck, one towel underneath me and another bunched in my arms as if to cradle a small animal. My shield from questioning. Eldest immediately wanted to see what I'd brought and was not disappointed to learn that what I had brought home was a personal shame they not dare repeat on threat of death. I threw those pants away. I loved those pants too. Jesus.

STILL OCTOBER 2026

We have a dog now. Little spindly thing who has been sulking along the edge of town. Eldest has been trying to catch him for months, setting traps, leaving small scraps of his breakfast in his pockets for whenever he sees the thing. As soon as I laid eyes on that animal, I knew Eldest would covet it like the prized gem centering a crown—the creature looks damn near exactly like the dog we had when he was younger, Greenie Boy. That dog looked like a puppy until the day he died at 8 years old. Eldest caught wind of the long-eared thing and could not let it go. And now we have a dog.

It whined for a while, but any time any person even thought about screaming at it Eldest was there, stepping between whoever and that damn dog. I didn't even think it liked Eldest all that much. What if it had a family? Babies or something? Were they out there too? But Eldest searched, taking the dog with him, albeit leashed so that it couldn't escape again. He found nothing, and the dog always returned with him tucked under one arm.

Eldest named him Squid Boy, but I just call it Dog. Dog is getting used to us, but he truly has taken a shine to Eldest (after weeks of forcing the issue. Probably some kind of Stockholm Syndrome shit). I haven't seen that kid smile so wide in years. So while Dog bugs me, cries in the night when he can't get back onto Eldest's bed (God, Dog is fucking stupid. Truly a marvel of stupidity), I have learned to accept his presence because he brings joy, genuine joy, to my kid.

Is it telling that I am already dreading the grief of Dog's death? He seems to be a younger pup, but it's all I can think about. The joy he brings can be smote any second, and I'm not sure if it'll have been worse for Eldest to have loved and lost, than to have never loved at all. I think whoever spoke that iconic phrase into existence, Shakespeare(?), was full of shit.

(undated)

I am sick today. Sick every day, probably. We had COVID in the before, which was quite the catalyst for many things, but now seems like such a distant, idiotic memory. It is likely another virus that cuts me off at the shins today, a mutant something laying siege to whoever manages to still cobble together a life. Who knows if it has a name, or if it ever will have one. We just call it, fittingly, the plague.

The kids each got it before me. Chills, fever, dry cough. All familiar symptoms. Nothing revolutionary aside from the swiftness and viciousness of it. Illness has ravaged our community, running in waves through the people, starting on the perimeter and now landing here. I can only assume the situation is the same everywhere else, or once was and now is here, or is here and will soon be there. The death toll is about 10% per our estimations. Ten fucking percent. A whopper of a death toll, aggravated by rampant starvation, lack of medical care, and poor hygiene. We implemented quarantine procedures, but they simply were not effective due to our housing issues. Too many people in one spot. A single infection begot thirty more just by going to bed to at night.

The whole thing is so reminiscent of COVID and yet somehow much less frustrating. At least now there is no illusion of assistance. We know no one is coming. No one is naming it. No one is tracking it. There will be no vaccine for us. It just is. And I feel like shit, although due to my unfettered access to the best this community has to offer, my chances of seeing the other side of this are better than most, and yet still they are fucking garbage. Our "best" is a before times now-homeless-former-pharmacist. They have the knowledge and zero resources.

Still, it is better than others, and I'll take what I can get. The kids bounced back after a few days. I can only hope I do too. They aren't miserable little drunks like me (that I know of) so one can only hope this virus appreciates bathtub hooch.

NOVEMBER TWENTY-SOMETHING, PER YOUNGEST, 2026

I haven't seen much of Youngest lately, but he came screaming at me this morning. Looked like he hadn't slept in days, eyes bloodshot and sunk. Might have been high. I grabbed him by the shoulders and shouted at him to shut the fuck up because he was rambling. Couldn't understand him. Eldest heard, tried to shoehorn his way between us—he wants to help so badly he doesn't notice his intrusion only lights the match. It was terrible. Youngest and I were tearing out throats. Eldest flattened himself against the wall as Aaron literally plucked Youngest off his feet until he quit talking. Kid sure has spunk but zero body weight. Anyway, after we stopped accusing each other of things, Youngest placed his sweaty, teenager hands on my cheeks and said, "I'm not high, mom. I found a way in."

To be fair, this only made him sound high. I should have been checking in on him more. I should be doing all the fucking things I said I would do as I razed the gutters. But I digress.

He takes me (and Aaron and Eldest) to his computer. We rigged him up a little something not long after the whole deal at the water facility. He refused to leave, and I needed to have some semblance of oversight into his wellbeing. Kid points to lines of code as if I have any understanding of the meaning, and says, "See?"

I tell him I don't know what the fuck I'm looking at, so he points again to a particular line. It says *TREASURY*.

I'm still not catching the meaning, but Eldest does. He keeps asking if Youngest is *for real*, and he nods and nods, finally explaining that he somehow hacked into the former City of Phoenix Treasury accounts. Banks accounts? I can only assume. I knew better, but a part of me got excited. Lottery excitement. Leverage excitement. But it didn't last, the accounts were cleaned out of all but some erroneous tenths of pennies here and there. The money wasn't the prize, though. He broke in. Countless before him already had. But now he had too, and all on his own.

I told him to call me when he found something worth a shit, and then immediately felt guilty for saying it. He was proud and I am his mom. So I poked him awake later while everyone was sleeping. He looked so tired. He hadn't slept. And I asked him how long it took him to break in.

Sixteen hours. That was it. I asked how long it would take him now, with everything he learned. He said thirty seconds.

Then I asked him why he showed me. I don't know what compelled me to ask that question. Maybe to assuage the guilt of what I was going to ask of him next. If he'd said, "Because I want you to be proud of me," well, I don't know what I would have done. I suppose I would have done the same thing. But he didn't say that. He said, "Because I want to help you."

Which I guess translates to *I want you to be proud of me.*

I told him he was brilliant, and I apologized for being mean earlier. Then I gave him a time to meet me after breakfast.

I fell asleep thinking of my dad and the crushing disappointment on his face as I fled that night, as our houses burned. How I probably watched from the mountain as he, my mom, my siblings, everyone, burned to death. I thought about how I would describe myself to him if he rolled up to the perimeter now, how I might show him around my fiefdom, what he might think of me. All the thought accomplished was a deep sense of relief knowing that will never happen.

I would have found them by now. They would have found me. Thank God for that.

(undated)

GODDAMN. I don't know how I recognized the man, but I did. Aaron thinks I'm nuts. I am nuts, but I am also in charge so fuck you, Aaron.

We went into town like we do on occasion. Went to Mimi's stall to get one of her biscuits. The woman is a national treasure, and her biscuits are delightful. Today we stood in line, which we do not usually do, but I was bored and not in a rush. To pass the time I stared at the neck of the man in front of me. He had a weird mole just below his right ear, probably cancerous by the looks of it, but who doesn't have cancer anymore? Some kid tried to dart in front of the line and this guy shouted at him. Not loud, but with that timbre that says, "I will fucking snap your neck if you take another step." Took even me aback.

I wouldn't have said a thing, would have just assumed this dude was having a rough go of it, but then he turned around, shoulders piqued, looking for commiseration and his profile stirred up a memory.

He was the dumpster rapist. The fucker that raped a drunk woman behind a dumpster but was lucky enough to be rich. The fucker that was called a promising young man while his victim was called a whore. It happened so long ago. It's not even a unique story. Didn't even happen in my state, but I remember his doughy cheeks (not even starvation could stiffen his jowls) and his wide, saucer eyes always turned up to the camera in feigned remorse. I remember how much I hated him because a friend of mine defended the guy. I lost that friendship, and I hated him.

And now he was unfortunate enough to land here—right in front of me at my favorite biscuit stall.

So I said to him, "I fucking know you."

And he spat back, "Yeah? Want a piece?" I mean, it just rolled out of him on impulse. The entire line stopped breathing. He clearly didn't know who I was. Must be new. How he even managed to survive so long is an affront to humanity. The universe is just toying with us now, and he was proof.

Clearly, he did not understand the hush. Aaron's spine shot rod straight, and he whispered that he just wanted a fucking biscuit. Too late though. The dude kept going, mistaking the quiet to be in the presence of him, not of me. So I let him go off. He got so red in the face, cheeks blown out and hot, and it was so comical in effect, so pathetic, that I laughed in his face. Eventually he called me a dumb cunt and stormed off.

Mimi looked genuinely ashy in the face over the confrontation. I could tell that she wanted to ask about it, but Mimi is smart enough to know when she should just stay out of dirty business. And because I like Mimi, I did not ask her if he comes for biscuits every day. I didn't indicate I cared at all. Aaron knew otherwise and was pissed. Said I ruined his breakfast with my temper. I apologized to him that night.

Now that I know the rapist is here, I'm going to make him pay for daring to exist, for no other reason than that I am angry. I am furious. And he will feel so good to ruin.

~~~

~~~

~~~

Well, I take that back.

I showed up to his room, no one else in tow, just me. Aaron didn't know what I was up to and was furious when he found out. Said I was being belligerent and obsessive, as if it wasn't those exact two qualities that started all this shit. He sure was fine with it then as I plotted coups against his friends and seized what he used to call his home. He was fine as he fucked me all the way to the top. Fine and dandy until I take a bit of initiative, satiate a craving without
~~~

making it his problem. He says it will always be his problem because he loves me.

The rapist would not be a problem. He was a coward and would piss his pants at the merest threat. You can always spot that kind of person, they are so obvious—so quick to name calling and bravado. Sure, sometimes a cornered animal might strike, but not this dumpster rapist. Not this guy. I just knew. And how right I was. When I appeared on the stoop of the shelter where he rented a room one of his roommates pointed out his door. He had no friends. No one to warn him, no one to save him. A few of them followed me, all too happy to see him go, which was when the triumphant sensation began to sour. This was no toppling of a predator. The was putting a bullet into the skull of some roadkill. I did not feel big anymore— I felt like an idiot.

The rapist swung the door to my knock as if he was used to being pestered, cocking his head to the side at the sight of me. One could literally witness the gears spinning as he reconciled our earlier meeting, finally recognizing my two faces—the one from the street and the one from his good common sense. His hands swung up in an instant.

"I didn't know," he shouted over and over again. But I wasn't there because he didn't recognize me. I was there to punish, and somehow this little worm stole the satisfaction from even that by being so pathetic. So I told him to sit down and tell a story. The story. I wanted him to tell me what he did to that woman.

He scoffed at first, insisted I just shoot him and end it because he wasn't interested in talking, but he was quick to recant as he breathed down the barrel of my willing pistol. I said to speak. So he did. And the story? It was revolting and yet anticlimactic. He had nothing to add which I didn't already know. His violations were nothing but bold, everyday newsprint. They were as average as any other violation. The rage that sent me there congealed into a lump in my gut. There was nothing to gain in that room, nothing that man could give me to make the trip worthwhile. There was nothing. And by the end of it he was sobbing, who knows why, certainly not for his victim I can tell you that much.

He might have lived if not for the dentist. For a split second this rapist's face mutated into the one who haunts me when I sleep, and once again he was lunging his body into me as I begged for treatment for someone I loved. I was back, and before I could think better of it, I shot that fucker in the head, residual brain and bone smattering his dirty bed sheets.

I saw then dentist again when I got home, only this time in the mirror.

FIVE

A mother runs into the desert alone. Her son, her life, everything fades into a hazy mirage at her back—a memory, a terror. She is about to wake up, but into what she doesn't know. She can hear them getting closer, the horsemen she summons, all named Death because she killed the rest of them. Death and Death and Death and her, a mother, running wild in the dirt, skin slippery, cheeks flush, bruising with life. Her boots kick up a furious wake until she can no longer compel them forward, so she drops to her knees, the earth's heat scorching her otherwise numb and calloused skin; it is just so hot—such a bad day to die.

Her son had screamed for her and still screams, she thinks. A wail she swears she can still hear even though that is impossible. She often checks to make sure he isn't following her. She might have to kill him if he is. Her other child is far away, or at least that is how she imagines him. Far away from here, safe, going to continue living. He will change his name out of necessity. There is no honor in her legacy. Her children must make a new one and pray that no one sniffs out the rot on their breath.

Jets bray above her, bringing their charge forward, guiding it toward their target. She is the target. The mother waves her arms over her head, a shipwrecked fool signaling to a military freighter, an ant of a creature.

"Here I am. Here!" she says. The engines drown her out, flying overhead and beyond, before dovetailing away on a dime.

Perhaps there is hope? Do jets fly so low alongside a bomb? Do they dare? It seems unwise; perhaps her son is wrong, and possibly his act was intercepted and diverted. Maybe they are saved.

But fate responds in the shape of displaced dirt bellowing into the sky by the tailwinds of her demise. The blast's shock yanks the mother's teeth from her skull as a bomb lands swiftly on the home she leaves behind

(undated)

Do you remember the abortion ban? Overturning Roe v Wade. I think everyone remembers it, not because everyone cared, not because they were against it, but because that's when we could no longer keep lying to ourselves.

It was too late, obviously. Too late to do anything about it. That's the armchair consensus from people who liked to lay their bodies down on that moral gauntlet. Too late to change things, sheep! We told you, we told you. And yeah, sure they did. But they didn't do anything else. And what they didn't understand was that their awakening was also a few decades too late. Rome fell incrementally—that monstrous, immovable beast does not get conquered from the outside. It does not get invaded. It gets greedy. An ouroboros consuming and consuming until it has nowhere left to turn but its own tail. Capitalism comes for everyone, and those siccing it upon us just hoped they'd be dead in their beds before it came for them too.

Let everything burn, but tomorrow.

Even now in our current state there exists a royalty. They fled DC long ago. Last I heard there was a billionaire bunker in Virginia. Not that the billionaires actually live there—they deserted the states the night before, knowing what was coming, knowing they'd caused it. They left us holding torches, bewildered, left for dead. The billionaire bunker is probably composed of a bunch of lucky tweakers. A stronghold for the few that got there first.

Last I heard, before our information pipeline was severed, was that our top ten percent had moved to South America. Brazil being a popular choice. Our president, who I sincerely doubt still breathes, but if he does, he's in Europe. Guaranteed.

They had to leave. They had to fucking leave. Because they torched the hill and the ants are pissed. They'll only return after we're finished eating each other, hurling salvation at us like gods, hoping to reinstate their posts on their manmade alters. Hoping we forgot or are too tired to stay angry.

They hope hope hope, hope for the rest of us, because we have none, never will again. Hope is for suckers and dreamers.

The only justice that remains is the systematic dismantling of their hope. Everyone's hope.

(undated)

I look at this dirt surrounding me, the filth and the dirt and the poverty and death, I look at it and try to stifle violence. A scream has been building ever since that day with the rapist. An unending atmosphere of grime clings to everything here. There is nothing to clean it. And here I am, finally the HBIC I always dreamed I would be, the head bitch of the hovel. Shoveling shit around and calling it a castle. And am I even in charge? In charge of what? Why do I cling to this title, this story I weave for myself, as my family dissolves between my fingers, as my past withers and dies alongside my future? I say "at least I running things" but to whom? Running things, myself, my kids, into the ground. I'm digging our graves. And for what? I'm playing pretend, little game of house in the kindergarten class while the teachers snigger over our toddler quarrels, who gets to be the dad today? And we shove each other into the little plastic kitchenette, the hollow fake plates go flying, a catastrophe in our eyes, but the teachers don't care because what silly things we are, such silly little babies with silly baby problems. My problem, all our problem, is that we were promised to grow up, to ascend to the same level of our teachers, to be in charge, but that was a lie. Look at me now. I spit on the other toddlers and pump my fists, oblivious to the raging city of wealth just beyond the fence for which I'm too small to see.

The rapist was a toddler. A fucking dumbass, and I felt nothing as I shoved his face into the forever sandbox. It's teacher that needs a lesson. I just have to figure out how to get to them.

I remember a joke from my early adulthood, something about how many toddlers you think you could beat in a fight. Toddlers or babies, can't quite remember now. It was the beginning of meme culture, of the destruction of civilization, because it connected us on the stupidest level. Regardless, I loved the joke. It was as stupid as I was, burning shit on the patio of the house I rented from my mom by pouring Bacardi 151 on old junk mail. We said shit like "I love the internet" and spent hours watching idiotic YouTube videos. We dumbed ourselves, cackling as we swirled down the drain. But even then, at our stupidest, at our most useless, the millions of us, even then we could smother and snuff out one adult. Millions of babies are enough to move mountains.

Just think about that.

WINTER (IT'S COLD AT LEAST)

I've been thinking a lot. Thinking is all I have time to do. It's all there is to do. I understand why humans used to war so much, the medieval sort of war with blades and blood and bodies fertilizing next year's crops. Good god, they were bored! You can't let a person think this much—the thoughts jut outward into the expanse, curiosity is piqued, people flourish in their imagination, but then as quickly as it sprouts and flies, the thoughts constrict. There is only so much one person can understand about the universe before it becomes too vast for them. We turn inward, constrict and contract, until we choke on our own contempt.

I've been thinking a lot more about the before time, lately. I don't know why. Sure, there is some yearning there, though less so for me. I do miss the comforts. The pettiness. The laughter. We laughed so much. What a treasure. It was easy to laugh then with so little else to occupy us. And yet I was such a belligerent little asshole then. Constantly put upon. Always stressed and tired and riddled with life-ending anxiety. Always pressed. But then I'd flee to the internet and see little glimpses of true horror. The real shit. The kind I live in now. And fuck me, I just could not *imagine* it. How could I complain when such nightmares exist? So I stopped complaining. I stopped doing anything productive because it could always be worse. And then, suddenly, it *was* worse. And I, all of us in the States at least, we were the ones that welcomed that lumbering demon into our beds. We said, "Here, take shelter for you must be exasperated from your toil, your calling of death. I am but a mere American, I know nothing of strife, so say the rest."

She did. I could say I am as miserable as ever now, but that would be a lie. The trauma lands like a tsunami, it transports you, crushes you, mangles you, but if you survive the tide, you are finally free, finally capable of understanding that there is so little in this world worth fearing. It quite simply isn't worth the time.

One could ask what they could have done with this mentality in the before times, they ruminate on it like a lovely little poem.

I guess this is what happens when people stop being afraid. Fear keeps compassion, empathy, and love afloat. Without it, we mutate into slobbering monsters. I suppose I'm just happy here, among the filth.

COLD

Eldest's dog died. The little thing he saved from the perimeter. Dog didn't die so much as someone killed it. It had gotten comfortable lately, yappy, and he kept the house awake. Aaron hated it, but I wouldn't let anyone take it away. Dog was Eldest's near singular bright spot, and now he's dead.

Eldest is bereft. He found the thing all smashed in the road, his tiny apple head caved in. He'd clearly been run over by a truck, not just struck, but smashed. Someone did this intentionally and meant for Eldest to find him. Aaron was white as a sheet, whispering to Eldest as he sobbed in a way I haven't heard since he was a toddler. This death has broken him.

Aaron immediately pulls me aside later, face purposefully slack when he's trying and failing to mask his concern. I knew he was thinking the same thing as me—no accident. A message. I don't know, am I insane? Is this a threat or am I just so used to seeing threats in everything that I make them up when they don't exist? But if it is and I ignore it, it could my kids under the tire of a truck next time. My kids. And how dare this fucker touch my kid, even indirectly, bring him this unwarranted pain when his only fault is sharing half my genetics? I'll burn this fucking city to the ground until the rat scurries out, I'll string him up by his tail and slit his throat, let him bleed out on the porch like bad meat. I'll find him. I swear it.

Aaron leaned in and whispered to me later that night, chin curved into his chest, begging me to be rational. I felt sorry for the man for having to deal with me, maintain me, calm my nuclear rage all the damn time. I suppose I should repay his patience by listening to him for once.

DECEMBER 2026

Youngest punched a kid in the face yesterday. That fucking dog is causing all sorts of issues. Eldest still is not himself. He wanders the town like a ghost, searching for something, his dog maybe? His old life, perhaps. An answer I think he is old enough to understand probably won't come, and if it does, will be another blow all on its own. No one claims the act— if it truly was a threat, they'd do well not to. But some smart mouthed kid, no more than ten, snuck up on Eldest on one of his walks for the mere purpose of taunting him. Called him soft, a pussy. Eldest didn't even cry when he relayed the news, just echoed the insults in a weird mechanical way that was, frankly, alarming.

Never saw Youngest coming with the retribution though. He is the cave kid, the one too much in his own head to see dirt on his shoes. He didn't even comment on it at dinner, just sat there like always, numbers spinning in his head, and went to bed. I hovered over Eldest that night, thinking of his dad, thinking this might all be too much for a kind soul like him. Worrying. Rubbing his hair only after he fell asleep. I used to say he had the same otter pelt hair as my husband, the kind that wicked away water in the bath. Thick and hearty. But now it was so soft, a few strands pulling up with my fingers because his hair is falling out from stress or grief or malnutrition or all of it. It just flickered something inside me that scared me. I have never in my life wanted to strangle a stranger's child to death more than that night, that nasty little shit, even though it wasn't this randoms kids fault that the dog was dead. Even if he was the one to kill it, a kid wouldn't do it without being bred to, without being steeped in something vile. But that didn't matter at that moment, didn't matter who built the scaffolding of the poison in this kid's heart, I wanted retribution and wow was this kid a great little target.

Not even I am that cold though.

Youngest, however, must have known who this was, went and found him the next day, and clocked him something fierce. The kid likely broke a bone when Youngest shoved him overtop a garbage can. And even though Youngest had many years on this kid, he wasn't all that much bigger.

This started the chaos, the mob rule of unfair retribution. Had he not been my son he probably would have been buried in an innocuous desert hole.

NEW YEARS

I want to build a nightclub. It's New Years Eve and we have nowhere to go. Wouldn't a nightclub be rad? Aaron is irritated. Says this is a huge waste of resources. It doesn't have to be though. Just four walls and some dope with a guitar will suffice, but Aaron knows me better than that. Four walls means twenty. A dope means a black-market sound system worth a week's supply of food. He knows, and I know, but I am not bending on this one. Most of the time I leave the financials—the "economy of our lives"—to him. He says yes, I go. He says no, I argue, but bend. Sometimes. But not on this.

Eldest still isn't right. Aaron keeps saying that Eldest doesn't want a nightclub, that it won't make him happy, and therefore won't make me happy, but he's an ostrich not seeing the bigger picture. Always one of his faults, if you ask me. I know neither of my kids want to dance. Maybe Youngest in the before times, when he was small and uninhibited, not this broken boy he is now. But now, no. However, what they do need is a group. They can't stay cooped up in their mom's bedroom, avoiding their peers and letting snotty ten-year-olds push them around. They can't learn from just me anymore. I wonder sometimes if I've already taught them everything I possibly could, that maybe now I'm just acting security until they're a little less stupid, but even so, they need friends. They need peers. Where do the kids go nowadays? The desert behind town is the only place I've ever seen them, poking holes with sticks and chucking rocks and shit. They need somewhere too.

I say all this, and Aaron's cheek inflame. It makes him angry. He says he knows what I'm doing, using the kids to force him into reckless shit. And, yeah, of course I am. He says I want the club. That I am the restless one, not the kids. Aimless. That I am becoming weird.

So what's the issue? Maybe this will help give me, the kids, the town, everyone something to look forward to, a place that makes surviving worth it. Blow off steam. I don't know. I think I'm trying to convince myself it's worth it.

Aaron admitted to me once that whenever I profess a plan to be in benefit of the greater good that he knows I am unsure. I wasn't exactly sure how to take that.

Maybe I can mull it over in my new fucking nightclub.

(undated)

Youngest needed to go to the doctor today. Of course, the doctor is less a doctor and more a former essential oils saleswoman who was in training to be a doula before the world exploded, but still she has more knowledge of the body than most anyone here (our former pharmacist died RIP). Whichever meds we are able to steal and horde, only she, myself, and Aaron can access. Still, I don't touch the shit without her. I need her to know that she is in charge and that access to healthcare as fair as I can make it. It's people like her that sow dissent when the bosses get sticky fingers.

Anyway.

Youngest had a fever. Treenie, the "doctor" gave him an antibiotic and some ibuprofen. She said his throat was raw. Might be strep, but who really knows. I have to say, she's gotten quite good at guessing. She's also watched a lot of kids die, although even Youngest is blossoming out of what we call a child and more into what we call a young man. Treenie gets extra cautious when my family stops in, and I think she worries I will kill her if something happens to my kids. I wouldn't, I like her despite her best efforts, but I think we all know just how fucking traumatic that would be. I'm rambling though. Rambling like always.

Youngest will be fine, whatever she gave him has already perked him up, but sitting in that little waiting room, aka her living room, I had one of those déjà vu moments where my entire being swore I had sat in that room before, in just that spot, in just that time of day, for just that reason. It's not uncommon for me have such thoughts, I have them more frequently than ever of late, but this one was potent. I thought perhaps I was losing my mind, maybe I'd already brought him here for this reason and got so high I forgot. Maybe all of them were just humoring me because they didn't want to deal with me, or because they are scared of me, and the thought of Youngest being so frightened of me that he would go to Treenie twice made me want to vomit. It took many hours for me to remember what triggered it, and when I did, I still felt like shit.

It was Treenie's couch. That weird, stained, green olive color fabric. The vaguely sterile yet old smell of her house. It triggered something from when Youngest was actually young, from before, when we had him tested for Autism et. al. He'd been struggling in school and the school didn't feel he needed assistance. He was struggling just like his dad struggled, and I knew enough about his dad to know it would not resolve on its own, he would not improve in school on his own, he needed help. I remember the waiting room of the testing facility, of little Youngest going back with the doctor clutching his bear stuffie, the same stuffie he lost when we fled. I remember him skipping towards me when he was done and hugging my neck and telling me he missed me even though it hadn't even been that long since he'd come out on a break. His reaction surprised me because he was never a child to express so much unless he really meant it, which meant he had been terrified and hadn't told me, and the relief of being done nearly brought him to tears. I remember his test going passed their closing time, and nurses filing out for the day while my son was still back with the doctor, and the anxiety and borderline rage I felt at their audacity to leave while my child was still stuck in a room.

We got his results a month or so later, after yet another round of tests, but then the world came screaming to its knees, at least my world did, and all those support systems I'd been trying to set up for my son evaporated into an angry mob, and well here we are.

There is still a lingering guilt over my failure. Much of it I can't control, but still, all that work and stress for this boy dissolved into uselessness so quickly. I suppose I never connected it to the "end of the before" until now, waiting in a dirty living room, hoping our retrofitted doctor will help my son, hoping this does not precede another collapse. It feels silly and superstitious to admit, but I can't shake the feeling something bad is coming, something worse than what has already happened.

I crawled into bed with Youngest last night. He didn't even wake up, and I was back in my own bed by morning.

SIX

A mother hides in the doorway of her home, her child a dot on the horizon far ahead. She watches him stagger away, the last of her babies. He is the final person to leave town, though not soon enough. He stumbles, falls, and she feels a shock of pain in her knees as if his stumble is her own, the earth lurching towards her, her grave finding her, bellowing with rage, screaming that she can't run anymore. Her son stands again, and the pain eases, but only a little.

Her palms still burn from the heat of his cheeks, her calloused grip clinging to him one final time. He needs to go, has to run, has to get the fuck out of here before running no longer means anything. The little voice in her head, so lethargic now, tick ticked ticking, too late already; she knows it is too late, but seeing him off was her last spot of rebellion. Her final cleave, the final little blade entering her chest, captures her heartbeat in a single stab of cool metal.

She did not speak as he fled, hoping her silence would soothe him, but still, his sobs followed him like a tailwind until he was too far away for her to catch the sound. His shirt is dirty. She wishes she'd noticed before he left. He shouldn't have to flee in a dirty shirt. His clothes should be crisp, ironed, and buttoned up to his neck like picture day. He should have food and water, extra socks, and sunscreen. Instead, she sends him into the seething desert with nothing but regret because they both know he won't need any supplies. Maybe he cries because his mother would never send him alone in the heat if she didn't intend for him to die there.

The mother wonders why she bothers sending him, knowing his feet can't possibly take him far enough, and she can't find an answer that makes sense. She does not want him to die, she doesn't want him to die in front of her, she can't bear the look in his eyes as it happens, as they perish, but none of these reasons excuse her choice. Dread drains the blood from her body; she is a stupid fucking fool; what has she done? Why why why why?

She screams for him, her boy still a spindly teenager. She screams for him until her throat rips apart. And she thinks that maybe he will stop, the little dot he has become. She thinks he stops just long enough to feel her guilt before molten death rains down upon them both.

JANUARY 22ND, 2027

I miss dancing, which is why I want a fucking nightclub, *AARON*. He'll cave, or else I'll go around him, which he knows, which makes him wild, gets him really screaming, honestly. But he will cave eventually.

I might have fucked up a bit though. I shouldn't have told him the real reason I wanted a club. Yeah, everything I said before about it being a release, good for the soul, something to live for, yeah those are still true. Maybe I didn't know exactly why I wanted one until I blurted it out across the table, laying centerpiece the truth from my past. The kids were there, which only made it worse. But I told him it reminded me of my husband. I can't remember the details, I might have blacked out, but I think Aaron dropped his fork. The kids, bless them, fucking noped outta there at the mere mention of their dad, as if his name was a treasonous chant.

Aaron sputtered out curses, accused me of wanting to sink town dollars into a ridiculous monument to my ex, which rankled the hell out of me, like my husband was some two-timing loser that stole my car and not the father of my children, my partner for decades, and, as much as I hated him when he was alive, the total love of my life. Aaron is a practical person, seems to understand the reality of things, but still, it bothers him to know with empirical certainty that he is not my number one, never could be. Or maybe he is just fucking tired of me, and this is just the slap in the face he needs to smother me with a pillow while I sleep.

But.

But I miss dancing. I only ever danced with my husband, usually while alone, just the two of us, the kids escaping up the stairs to slam their doors in attempts to drown out our loud music. We liked electronica mostly, but also pop-y classics, anything that got the body moving. We hovered between rooms of the house, dancing in unison but never together, drinking, getting high on fruity edibles because smoking was too much for me. We moved, we sweat, we hollered until the commotion was too obnoxious to continue. Our marriage was tumultuous, toxic most of the time. The mere sight of him would induce panic attacks for me, something I never told him. Even now, whenever that sensation rolls throughout my body I think of him, look over my shoulder for his ghost. And it wasn't all his fault. It was ours, together. Something we made, something we built, and then we took turns shoving each other from the cliff's edges onto spikes of our own, homegrown neuroses. We were fucking maniacs. But dancing was one thing we did well together. We both lacked any coordination, not a spot of talent between us, but fuck, a person doesn't need to be talented to enjoy something. And we enjoyed dancing.

Aaron likes to dance too, but it isn't the same. He likes to hold me close, clutch at me. Not in an oppressive way, but in a sensual way that only exacerbates how different we are as people. At least to me it does. I wonder if he even knows quite what I am feeling. Does he sense it too? Are all men who love women this oblivious? I thought it was only my husband, but maybe not. Maybe it's not even men, maybe it's me? But that's silly. That's just me projecting this aura of mystery upon myself as if that makes me better somehow, when the mystery is probably just a veil of confusion so thick you could choke on it.

Anyway, Aaron doesn't want a club. I don't know why he is threatened by a ghost. Maybe it's because *I* am. The lingering visage of my husband is one of the only things to scare me anymore. Does that make the club more a grave? A cemetery to lay him to rest, and probably me with him once I go. Maybe that's what worries Aaron.

Still, the worry won't stop me. It hasn't yet, anyway.

115

(undated)

I crashed the razer today, or, I crashed what we call the razer. I was drunk and racing some junkyard dogs. I should have known better because it fucked up my old back injury from when I was rear ended in the before time.

The guy sped off (after rear-ending me), but someone chased him down and forced him to pull over. Then once that good Samaritan left, the guy drove off a second time. The impact tweaked my back, and I never did manage a good night's sleep after it. The guy was never caught, but I sleep a bit easier now knowing he's likely dead. Not that he was inherently a bad person, whatever that means, just uninsured or something, but he hurt me. It was his fault, and I was crying, and then he just...left.

What stood out though were the solid amount of people running to help. I remember feeling oddly comforted by it, even though I was scared and pissed and shaken. People checked on me. People gave a shit.

Besides the guy that caused it, I'd say the least interested person for my safety was the actual cop, because as he was walking back to his car he spun around real quick like "Oh I forgot, are you okay?" and when I said yes he turned right back towards his car even though I was still finishing my sentence. Didn't even have the time of day to hear the period at the end. I cried in my car until my husband showed up.

Now, when I crash shit, people laugh. We are all drunk, so it's fine, but if they don't laugh, they watch. They watch close. Gotta see if I'm still breathing, still able to make decisions. There are a few people who would cover my mouth and plug my nose under the guise of CPR if they thought they could get away with it. No one comes to help anymore, and I honestly don't blame them, but it does make me sad. It shouldn't, I probably don't have a right to be sad, but my kids see it, you know? They see the indifference, or maybe even the hope. They learn to keep their heads down and mouths shut, they absorb our frail community into their bones, now so weak they haven't enough marrow to build something new.

We keep saying dumbass shit like "We fight so our kids can live." But will they even know how? We are teaching them to survive, steeping them in desperation and suspicion and death, and that shit infects the soul. It curses the blood, I think. I don't know how many generations it takes to be free of the curse. Probably a lot of people smarter than me with better answers, people who know this intimately, how corruption stains and just never leaves the body, no matter how many times removed.

Why, really, are we doing this to ourselves? Why do *I* do it? Sometimes I think it would be easier to just crawl into a hole and die, so instead of that I grab a handle of bathtub hooch, hop into the razer, and race dogs just to see which of we things gives up first.

IT'S BEEN 100 YEARS... OR MAYBE IT JUST FEELS THAT WAY

I haven't written in so long. Why should I have? There is nothing to document that I wish to remember, but I can't help but feel the pull to do something. SOMETHING. I only write when I'm desperate, it seems. I guess I have always been a desperate person.

I wish I still had the old journals of years ago, back when the kids were still kids, back before Aaron died and Eldest left. I just let him go too. I don't even know where he is. He said he hated who I was, that he couldn't stay or else he'd hate himself. Hate me or not, he's only alive because of me. At least he is alive to hate me. This sentiment feels reminiscent of another entry, something from long ago. Seems I have a way of things.

Youngest is quite young man now. Suppose he is now my only, considering Eldest has renounced me entirely. I feel ancient calling him a hacker, but that's what he is. He lives and breathes on the computer.

He's rewired the entire house, rigged up cameras, and now spends his days seeing just how much shit he can break. He's gotten quite good. I don't know if that's skill or just lazy internet securities considering the state of affairs in the US right now, but either way it works to our advantage. Youngest says shit I don't understand, often talking over and beyond me, shit about servers and localized something, how he's created a small bubble internet just for us. I ask how secure it is, and he says it's secure enough for anyone stupider than he is, which is most of us, but that also makes him the lord and savior of all our communications. Aaron hated this, said I gave too much control and afforded too much trust in a child, and he wasn't wrong, but Aaron's dead now. So it's me and Youngest. I know he hides things from me—for all his smarts with coding and God knows what else, he is the most useless at reading humans. Quite terrible at it. I don't tell him how often I pick up on his little lies simply because I don't want him to get better at it. I need him to think he's pulled the wool over me, and, yes he does, but not as efficiently as he thinks. That's my only card with this fucking kid.

Every night we both sit at our table meant for four, passing machinations between us. I find it curious how each of us seem to gather such similar information, yet by completely different means. When Socks was fucking his neighbor, Youngest found their messages. I heard the mistress whimpering at the stands about how his wife had broken one of her windows in a rage. We made a game of it, though we haven't played it in a while—we called it 'who knew first'. I won almost every time, even though Youngest had all the information first, he just didn't know how to interpret it. Or he was lying, giving me the delusion of control. Or I'm overthinking it, getting paranoid. Or all of the above.

At this point it's probably stupid to start another journal. It's like the key to the cipher—could be cracked by anyone, could take me down. But I think everyone is plotting to take me down, because they are, it's only natural. I guess I'm trying to explain something to myself here, if only I understood what. I guarantee the answer will come only once it's far too late to make anything of it. Seems to be my only way of operating. Time will tell, I guess.

(undated)

Aaron wasn't the first man I thought might kill me, but he was the only one who might have actually done it. In the months before he died, I would catch him standing at the foot of our bed, just staring. We were so in tune with one another at one point that I refused to believe that he did not know I was awake, watching back. He had to have known, said I often snored like a lumberjack, that for such a routinely withdrawn person while awake, I let it all out when I slept. So, he must have known that I was watching him back, eyes closed all but a sliver, searching for shifting shadows, waiting for his heartbeat to change, anything to signal he'd finally had enough of me. But the moment never came. He'd crawl back into bed, and I'd fall asleep again. Neither of us spoke about these night terrors. Neither of us dared break whatever silent pact we'd made. I figured if anyone was to finally kill me, it'd make sense to be him. But, boy, he'd have to work real hard to succeed.

Illness eventually took him, just like my husband. It hit me like a bad case of déjà vu, watching him wither and die, wondering what was eating at him while I remained unscathed. For Aaron, it was his body that finally collapsed on itself, toppling top to bottom like a cave in an earthquake. Perhaps cancer or some other odious disease. The doc administered every potion in her arsenal, but it couldn't touch whatever he had. I'd heard of a settlement in old Phoenix with a working hospital, obviously a scaffold of its old self, but a hospital. Aaron refused to go, said he'd die at home thank you. I didn't argue with him. I doubt he'd have survived the trek, and to be honest, I wasn't sure what home would await me upon our return.

My husband left us in the before. Guilt burrowed into me like a parasite after he passed. To this day I wonder if I'm the one who killed him, wrecked him, took his malleable soul into my iron fists, and simply squeezed the life out of him. No one can ever measure up to my steel resolve, so said Aaron anyway. My husband, I think, would have lived had we divorced. I should have divorced him. We were a toxic pair, only I was much more difficult to break. I had to be. We had children to raise, and he sure as fuck wasn't gonna do it. We were so finely attuned to one another's weaknesses that we shaved each other into blades, made weapons of each other in the name of survival. We should have seen that only one of us would make it out alive. He should have known it would be me. He should have left, but he would rather have died begging for my scraps instead. God knows I treated him more like a mangey stray than a partner, towards the end at least.

I asked him once in therapy that if he truly believed all the things he said of me, why on earth would he stay with me? Why be married to a person you think such harsh things about? Why not run? He only said, "Because I love you." I said he was more afraid of being alone than anything, and that was the only reason he stayed. I honestly can't recall how he responded to that, but I remember feeling helpless.

I hate marriage. I will always hate it. If anything comes out of the implosion of civility as we know it, I hope it's the cultural death of marriage. What a goddamn crock. What an utterly useless function of society. Marriage is a soul killer. Humans are not meant for it. Not that we aren't meant for relationships, or partnerships, or love, or sex. But marriage is an insidious construct that serves no purpose but to trap and kill. It's a bear claw in the woods, and it leaves you missing limbs, dripping blood in the dirt until you finally just die to get it over with.

If one of my sons wishes to take a wife or a husband or whatever, I will lose my fucking mind. I don't think I have much choice in the matter anyway, but still, that alone might end me before anything else.

(undated)

I remember words like emotional blunting. I don't know why I remember them. I shouldn't. They are stupid, useless words now, not something worth committing to the wasted folds of my brain, and yet it endures beyond the grief and the guts and trauma. Trauma is another word I loathe. Trauma became a weapon to be wielded by every moron of the internet from before. Are we not going to discuss the trauma of watching our mothers do dishes? The trauma of your parents never buying you dunkaroos or dungarees or whatever insipid thing? Absolute gibberish, and yet I'm still mad about it. Why am I mad about it? Why do dead people still bother me? Probably because I am alive, and if a person is alive, they must be irritable. To continue living is an act of spite if you ask me.

The term emotional blunting arrived in my lexicon during a particular trying time in the before. I was googling shit, wondering on the reasons I felt so removed, so numb, why my hair was falling out, and when all that shit would stop. The answer was about as depressing as the symptoms, but the term stuck for some reason, landing like a cudgel on my psyche. You see this? I am BLUNTED you mother fucker. The mother fucker in question being my husband. I am thinking about him more and more lately, imagining Eldest fleeing into his soft arms, the arms of parent that hadn't gone feral. He always tried much harder than me to be kind, even when he failed or fell or fucked up, he tried with much more sincerity than I could ever pretend to be a kind person. This is why I felt like such a deranged human for wanting to leave him. Felt broken, like my desire to flee wasn't appropriate and anything that happened afterward would be my fault, like I deserved to drown and drown and drown until I was dead for daring for a different life, even if it wasn't a better life, just different. This is funny to me now, and I chuckle even writing it.

I suppose I remember these things because they are not new. Perhaps more powerful, but insultingly common all the same. Distress doesn't happen to the few—it happens to the living, period. I feel blunted again in the wake of Eldest's departure. I feel nothing. I want to be furious, I want to cry. I will myself to the action, to prove I am human still, that I have not irreparably mutated beyond saving, but nothing comes, and while this should cause even more distress, it simply...doesn't. I feel nothing. I don't even miss him. I should, logically, be stricken with grief, but I'm not. I think my body understands something my brain does not—to fold into this loss would end me, and so it cauterizes the feelings from my brain, some cortex or other. Only when enough time has safely passed will the emotions come. If I even live that long

(undated)

I keep seeing dead people. This time at the end of the hallway. I saw my dead husband. Spouse, as I'll call him here for brevity's sake.

It was dark, not even a shadow to be seen, but I saw him. I saw the outline of him, his silhouette haunting the blunt end of the wall. Just staring at me. There was no mistaking who it was. Dreaming, I thought, had to be dreaming. So I dug my nails into the meat of my bicep, bringing blood back with me. Not a dream, I guess, or if so, a really fucking scary one.

Funnily enough, Spouse used to have those kinds of dreams. Waking dreams. Nightmares. He screamed in my face once as I leaned over him. This was before we were married, still sleeping in my childhood room at my parent's house, pretending to be grown. I leaned over him, probably because he was making some kind of whimper, I don't even remember now, and he screamed at me. Told me he'd had a nightmare where he'd woken up to me leaning over him in just that way, over and over again, and every time my face mutated into a monster. Another time he charged at me, running top speed because I'd forgotten something before work and had come home to get it. Whatever I'd forgotten was in the bedroom, and he'd been in the middle of the dream, thought I was an intruder, and charged, all while moaning this bizarre dream sound. He didn't stop until he was directly in front of me, now fully irritated (we had been married a while by then), me asking what the fuck he thought he was doing.

Anyway, I checked on Youngest to see if this person I was seeing was him, but found him asleep at his computer. Again, a piece of my gut evaporated, and I knew something was wrong. This visage resembled Eldest, he always did look like his dad, but it wasn't Eldest. I'd know the jut of his chin anywhere, in the dark, in a dream, in a crowd of a thousand people. I know my kids.

This was Spouse, and there was a reason he'd begun to haunt me. I wanted to scream all over again WHAT THE FUCK ARE YOU DOING but just as I opened my mouth to speak his shadowy head turned on a swivel, aimed intently in the direction of Youngest, arms sprung out like spiders' limbs and he vaulted up the wall, skittering away before I could stop him.

Then I snapped out of it by Youngest shaking me much in the way I'd shaken him a few days ago. His voice seemed so small again, like a kid's voice. Like the Youngest in the before. I'd scared him badly, and when I answered him, a curt "What?" he started to cry.

I wonder if he saw his dad that night too. I'm still too afraid to ask.

TIFFANY MEURET

(undated)

I thought I saw Spouse again today, only it wasn't him, it was Youngest. My heart stopped so abruptly that began to cough. I think that cough is the only reason my heart started again.

Youngest came running up to me, wild, eyes fuckin saucers. He was rambling about something, and maybe it was the cadence of it, the way he put his words together, but suddenly he became Spouse. His dad. I felt like he'd returned from the dead, a tired, broken angel or something, and that he had come to finally kill me for everything I've done. I was also stricken by the sudden thought that Eldest was dead. I couldn't shake it, and once I stopped coughing, I vomited, and once I finished that I screamed until Youngest stopped talking. I don't remember what I said, but by the time I faced Youngest again, wiping the barf from my chin like a drunk stumbling from a dark alley, he looked like himself. Still the little boy despite his acne and sparse facial hair, despite being what many would call a young man. He was him again, hand on my shoulder, babbling still about something he had found, oblivious to my completely insane reaction.

Took me a few minutes to get him to slow down so I could understand. He kept saying, "I think it's real," repeating it on loop. I asked him what was real, and he said, "The codes."

Codes. Just kept saying codes. He wasn't making any sense. I didn't care about codes, or any obscure place of the internet he'd wrenched from the shadows, but then he said the word bombs. Bomb. The bomb.

I still didn't totally understand, but I was paying attention now. I asked what bombs. He said nukes. I laughed in his face. Fucking idiot kid thinking he simply "hacked" his ignorant ass into skeleton remnants of the government and found the codes to nuclear missiles. I told him as much, reminding him that if he found it, others must have too and long before him, and if it was even real, they likely didn't work, and if they were still active codes, then there couldn't possibly be any bombs left that haven't been sold to our companion fascists countries.

Youngest nodded, eyes glazed, adrift in his head. I could tell he didn't believe me, he never does when I douse him in reality, so I grabbed him and shook him hard enough to snap a baby's neck. Told him to stop fucking around in dangerous places. Leave it alone.

Told him I'd kill him myself if he kept on with it. But he didn't believe that either.

I wrote him off, grabbed a handle of booze and went to bed while calling him a daydreamer, and laid awake until morning, an untouched bottle cradled in my arms.

It couldn't be true, of course. Logic decrees it.

It just can't be real.

(undated)

I'm dreaming of him. Why am I dreaming of him again? Still? Why?

I can't help but consider it portentous that my husband has resurrected himself to me. I see him everywhere, wake up screaming as he looms over my bed, as I know I am sleeping, as I can't move. I wander the house, so quiet now, this machine of a house so full of sullen, tired people, and I see him in the shadows, whipping out of sight the second I face him. I see him hunched over Youngest the way he used to when he would help him with his math homework. I was never great at the math stuff, though I could have helped if I tried, I just didn't want to. Fuck math and all that. I see Spouse pointing at the screen, one clawed hand gripping Youngest's shoulder. The glow of the screen dies on Spouse's skin, as if he is a black hole absorbing it all. Youngest's hair lifts from his scalp, drawn into the pull of it, and I scream and scream thinking he might disappear like his brother. Then I wake up.

I don't know why I am dreaming like this now. Or maybe I do, I just refuse to say it aloud, won't even write it as if the definition would give it power. I am becoming superstitious to a delirious degree. I don't think I am the same. I know I am not the same, no one would be after everything that has happened. The problem is that I can no longer explain myself to myself. My actions operate outside of my logic, and I can't piece them together anymore. I think I am slipping, and Spouse is here like a nail in a coffin. A threat. An answer, I suppose.

I think he is telling me that I am close to home again. Every night I wait for him to extend a hand. I don't know what I will do when he does.

(undated)

Purgatory fucking sucks. That's where I am now. Between things. The before is no longer the before—it's a fucking memory. A bedtime story.

I keep dreaming of dead people—they're rotting, eyes popping out of sockets, looking at me with confusion as if they want me to explain what is happening to them, as if they don't know they are dead. I catch glimpses of my children in these crowds of ghosts—bits of them as they are now, an arm, the collar of a shirt, and bits of them when they were little, like a laugh or a smile, but then I reach for them, the thing that looks like my kid, and it's missing its eyes entirely. I say it instead of he or them because it isn't human, whatever it is. This is the shit people mean when they talk of demons. There is no hell, only our own deteriorating minds screaming for absolution. A purpose. And knowing completely that one will never come because we've fucked it all up. I've fucked it all up, and now I am here.

I am distressed, a mote in a fog, a pissed off little gnat with a Molotov cocktail in each of my insect limbs, and every time I go to chuck one off the fog laps over me like a wave or a heavy blanket. Snuffs out the flame, the smoke, snuffs out all the life in me. But fuck if I'm not pissed enough to light those wicks all over again.

Youngest startled me this morning as I raged to myself in the hallway. Just him and I live in this house now, the rest left. I think I frightened them. I honestly don't even know what is happening outside the walls of my house. Neither youngest nor myself ever leave. Food, booze, all the things needed to keep me placated are delivered without fuss. I am not even a figurehead anymore. I too am a ghost of who I used to be. People scream at night, sometimes just outside my window. I don't know why, and I have no inclination to ask. I assume I'll get a bullet hole for my trouble. Not like there is anything I can do to help anyway.

Once the appearance of status quo no longer holds any power, I can only guess that Youngest and myself will have our heads on a pike to usher in the new order through the front gates of my former home.

Youngest keeps talking about bombs. I don't bother to stop him anymore. Blow it all up baby doll. Blow all of it up.

SEVEN

A mother cradles an empty space, hands curled around a newborn head she can now only see in the dark as her mind wanders. Her son does not want to see his baby, so she, the grandmother, scurries into the darkness, the boy child wriggling against her breast as he aches for food, for his mother. The baby does not know his mother is dead or that he is held by the person who killed her.

Jennie is his mother. This mother wonders what Jennie would have done had she lived. Had Jennie lived, this baby would be a statistic like the rest. At least now he has a chance, however brutal the price. This mother wonders if her grandson will thank her or curse her for paying it on his behalf. It's likely, though, that he will never know.

She delivers the baby with a journal bundled into his blanket. Her most precious items were all together

—so fragile and easily lost. Her heart feels empty without them.

Back at home, her son places a sweaty hand on her shoulder. He does not speak, and she is glad for it.

The bomb will speak for them all, anyway.

(undated)

Grief is a funny thing. Not haha funny, but funny as in odd. Confusing. I have felt grief many times in my life, and each time it hits like something new, something I've never felt before, as if this is the first time we have ever met. The potency of grief is astonishing. Not like rage, which slips on like an old glove. Rage is familiar, and in a way, easy. Simple. I understand rage better than most, let it light me like a furnace, keeps me functioning when every other element of my life is actively trying to kill me. Choo-choo mother fuckers, I've got fury on my side and you better get your silly ass off the tracks and out of my way.

Grief doesn't operate like that though. I wonder if other animals feel grief like humans do? I can't imagine the sentiment is exclusive to humans. I remember hearing about orca mothers wailing for their calves after they were taken to a different aquarium or sea park, or dogs that wait for years for their dead or missing owner, shit like that. It must be grief. Only grief has the power mutate a creature so ferociously. Rage can act like that, but it is more a mask for much more debilitating emotions. Probably why I am usually so angry.

(undated)

The exhaustion part of this has set in. I'd forgotten about the exhaustion, how the adrenaline spikes at the mere hint of bad news, followed by a pandemic level crash that sweeps your sense of self off its feet. When I say this, I mean life. I don't know why I felt the need to specify that, or to who, as I am the only one reading this garbage. Maybe I think I'll forget what I meant because I do that a lot. I used to write poetry. Very dumb poetry about divorce and grief and whatever, as if I knew those felt like. Maybe I did, because Spouse had died, and I thought that was the worst thing that would happen to me in my life. I wish I'd had the presence of mind to understand that everything, always, can get worse. Though I suppose one must live a worse life to know it, and is there ever an end? Does it always get worse? Or is there a bottom, one singular creature peering at the rest of us, eyes lit up like a cat, all green and judgmental, screaming "This is the bottom, you dumb fucking slut!"

I'm probably being dramatic. I do that a lot too.

Youngest doesn't eat anymore. Neither do I. We both drink coffee with a little bit of protein powder in it, at least that's what I assume it is. We can't sleep. We don't want to sleep. Now both of us are seeing ghosts. Youngest doesn't see his father like I do. He won't tell me who he sees. I asked if it was Eldest and he kind of shook his head in a way suggesting he knew I'd say that, and so he knew he needed to deny it before I lost whatever remained of my fucking mind. Then again, he could have just been strung out like I am, not sleeping. We need to sleep, we keep seeing shit and not sleeping only makes that worse. Spouse's neck is so long, like a comic book character but without any of the whimsy. He seems so tired, like his head is too heavy, and the mere act of keeping it atop his shoulders is too much, so it stretches as it lolls towards the ground, gravity stealing all the firmness of his spine. His eyes are dark empty sockets. He fiddles with things in the dark. I hear him whispering shit, gibberish mostly, like he's speaking to himself in his sleep. It reminds me of when he used to play games on his phone—so intent on something, muttering about stats I didn't understand, occasionally yelping with frustration or success. It's like that but fucking haunted and creepy. I yell at him to go away, but then he freezes, which is much worse than the muttering, and sometimes turns to stare at me. When he does that, he doesn't stop. Just stares and stares, getting closer to my face every time I blink, until he's right there, two black, nightmarish orbs watching me silently, a challenge.

I close my eyes so I don't have to see him, but I can't sleep. The sensation of being watched buzzes around me and it's loud. Too loud. Sometimes I can only sleep to the sound of muttering. Sometimes I wake up and it's Youngest muttering, just like his Dad in my nightmares. I don't even know what's real anymore.

I don't think he does either.

(undated)

I used to say that the worst thing about writing was the authors. I stand by it to this day. Fucking creatives huffing their own goddamn farts, thinking they are changing the world with their pen or keyboard or whatever they use. Thinking they are special, delusional to the fact that any creative field (but especially writing) is a trade. It is just a trade. Just because you got your own feelings mixed into it doesn't mean it is any grander than being a plumber, which, you'll love to know, is a far far FAR more valuable and desired trade lately. To call a trade "a calling" is a travesty, because it makes you insufferable, stupid, and frankly, makes it impossible for you to create good art. A writer with "a calling" is a toddler with a binkie.

What do I bring to anything with my words? Catharsis for me, yes. But that is it. I could have gone to therapy and gotten better advice. Probably should have. I think of these things while I scribble in my little book. There are four of them now. Four journals. I left one in a bathroom years ago now, only half full, hoping someone would pick it up and be inspired by me. I can hardly bear to admit this even to myself. This was back in the days of me signing each entry as The Woman, a signifier so asinine I can barely speak it. Only I know of this, and should anyone point it back to me I'll deny it, but they won't, because that journal is long gone now. Someone probably used it to wipe their ass or for kindling or something. Done something useful with it. But that's not why I left it there. I thought I was some kind of master of the realm, a little spitfire trash rat cutting throats and winning. Mad Max wannabe idiot with blood on the brain. I was the resistance. The counterculture. I had a calling.

This is the only journal I still own though. I think Eldest took the others because I've never been able to find them after he left. I hope he burned them.

Now I walk outside my front door hoping to touch grass and finding only filth. My fault, I know. One child gone, another wasting away in front of me, delirious, nightmares, ghosts.

Bombs. He keeps talking about bombs. I wonder what would happen if we tried to shoot one off?

Send us all to our maker. There's no point breathing anymore.

(undated)

There's a cat that keeps coming around. I thought I was imagining it at first, but then Youngest mentioned it. Looks like a tiny calico tabby mix—very ballsy and slightly stupid. The thing sprints across the hallway chasing imaginary somethings, crashing into walls like a banshee before disappearing somewhere in the house, never to be found until it is ready to be found. I think it is a girl because most calicos are female, but who knows? Could be the weird, sterile 1% that ends up being male.

At first, I thought it was Spouse again with his spider arms scuttling through the house. I would lock myself in my room when I heard it, terrified of his black eyes settling upon me, muttering with even more limbs. I couldn't bear it, but then I heard this tiny mew, and there was this cat. We stared at each other for what seemed like minutes before she turned on her kitty heels and scaled the drywall before disappearing. I hadn't seen a cat in ages. Honestly, I can't remember the last time I'd seen any feral creature. Not since Eldest and that pup. I think people were trapping them and killing them, eating their meat. Makes sense. I am not sure if it is a good sign or a bad sign that the animals are returning. It could mean that the people are satisfied, fed, and not compelled to kill anything that moves. Could also mean that the people are dying so the animals feel brave again. I'd have to leave my house to know one way or another and I'm not sure I want to do that. I need to sleep. I need to appear healthy or else whoever remains will tear me limb from limb. They'll crush me if they think they can, and I look like a waif, a skeleton, and crazed inhuman thing with a train of ghosts on my heels. There is no safety out there, not after Aaron died. I didn't realize how much he protected me, insulated me from rebellion. People *liked* Aaron. They villainize me. I suppose I am a villain. I don't know why I am still alive. Maybe they think I am already dead, or at least effectively dead. I don't know if I have any allies left. Maybe I am going nuts? Or have I always been nuts? Who gets to be the arbiter of being nuts? Certainly not the crazy people, but then how does one know if they are crazy without being told?

The cat's back. I see her eyes under the door. Bright green things. Perfect. Cat eyes just have a depth that is missing in other animals. Something godly about them. Maybe I'm just crazy?

(undated)

Do you know what it feels like to be broken? I feel like I've written about this before, I've certainly been broken before, sad, all those things. This is new though, although it would have to be new to even register. Lack of sleep doesn't help, and when I do sleep, I see things, and if I close my eyes to not see them, I hear them. The cat keeps pawing at my door until I finally let her in to sleep with me. She nuzzled up right by my face and I sobbed into her fur. I don't know why. Or, I guess I know, I just can't articulate the emotion. I think I might already be dead, and this little green-eyed kitty is here to usher me somewhere else, away from here, but I won't go. Why won't I go? Shouldn't I want to? Even Youngest will be better off in the end. I don't know if he even knows I am here. I went looking for him the other day and for some reason I was expecting to find a child. I kept seeing his gigantic child eyes, the way he looked when he would come back into the house after swinging in the yard for hours. He used to love to swing, and I would always look at him and think he was so skinny, he never did eat much, but he was so skinny because he just never stopped. Even still, watching his tablet, whatever, his mind was always racing and going, he was always going. His brother would hover over him like a smaller, irresponsible surrogate mother, knowing this kid would wander into traffic at any moment, and if there wasn't any traffic he would seek some out just to crash into it. I kept seeing that little face I used to call skinny and was met with the gaunt, sunken visage of what he is now. What I made him. I might have shrieked if I had any energy left, but instead I stared at him like a stranger, then later sobbed into a cat. My babies are gone from me. My babies are gone.

This cleave inside me is unbearable. It's probably why I used to stay so busy. My mind and me left alone are toxic, like my body releases a poison when I think too much. I steep myself in it like bad tea, until it gets scummy and cold. And then I cry, leeching away the liquid so that the poison just concentrates. What am I to do then? Each emotion pressurizes me more and more and more. Shit is bad. I cannot keep going on like this.

EIGHT

A mother leans into her diary, scribbling furiously with her half-dry pen. She writes words over and over again, hoping the imprint of the ballpoint will transfer her message when the ink fails. Occasionally, she lifts her head above the pages to scan the room. If asked for what, she will not be able to answer. Shoulders curling protectively over her pages, she returns to her writing.

A wail sounds from a deeper space of the house. The mother does not notice. Again, it repeats, more pitched than before, but the mother does not lift her chin nor her eyes, does not allow the pen to slip her wretched grasp for even a second. Nothing penetrates her echoing thoughts, nothing.

Screams now, a shout. The house begs for her to notice, yet the mother refuses. She grunts a low dissent without even pursing her lips as if to say, 'not now.' But the house does not wait, and neither does her son, who soon comes crashing through her door with violent intent.

He screams to her, for her, at her. MOTHER, he says in indecipherable tones. MOTHER LISTEN.

The mother freezes, palms slick from the fury of her writing, denying any further acknowledgment of his interruption. Her gallow-eyes remain dark.

I FIGURED IT OUT, her son says. I FUCKED IT ALL UP.

Well, of course, he did, she thinks to herself. The mother knew this moment was coming, hoping she might be able to finish her entry before it struck, but alas, the world waits for no one.

She lingers on a word, gazing at how her hand created it, how the thought congealed in her mind, instructing her muscles, her fingers, and the strung-out tendons of her hands to duplicate that thought onto a page. But was it a duplicate? Can a mind be duplicated? A recreation, perhaps an interpretation. Never mind, it does not matter anymore.

MOTHER, DID YOU HEAR ME? Her son continues. DID YOU HEAR WHAT I SAID?

And she does hear, nodding an affirmation to get him to stop talking. She listens, child. She knows.

IT WILL LAND ON OUR HEADS.

Yes, it will, she thinks—all the better.

WE MUST RUN.

The mother will do no such thing, yet she won't fault her son for trying. If he must run, he chooses to die in the desert instead of at home. Perhaps this is better. The mother would rather die anywhere but this forsaken and empty house, but her body doesn't have the strength to rise from her seat, let alone to run. Running is for the young. She might not be what others consider old, but she is long past her expiration.

The mother tightens her grip on her pen, and the son understands. He nods. He will not run without her. Then he disappears into the dark bowels of their home, back to where he has lived for years, back to his nest of wires and screens, watching a radar tracker beep the tune of his death.

The mother writes until her fingers become ash.

(undated)

Why do I write? Why these journals? Back in the before I was diagnosed with OCD. I refused the diagnosis at first, no way I had anxiety or some weird obsessive problems, even as I obsessed over the diagnosis and what it meant, as I stayed awake at night thinking of the mat on the back patio and how dirty it was, how I wanted to burn my house down because the floors were covered in dog hair and I'd just swept, and I checked my breasts for lumps even 15 minutes until I was sure I was dying, as I stewed in a rage that I couldn't yank myself free from, as I obsessed and obsessed and obsessed. I think this is why I write though. I obsess. I'm a late stage philosopher, the kind I always hated in school because they are so fucking abstract they had clearly abandoned reason, talking about chair or something and whether chairs are real, even if you can touch it, is it real? What does real mean?

I mean, jesus fuck bruh, go get laid. Touch grass. I don't know. You are centering yourself in an endless vortex of your own creation where nothing matters, real is never real, consequences-*who are they?*- where humanity is nothing but a collection of miraculous atoms, energy swirling and swirling. We are nothing. Life is nothing.

And that's where I am. I used to think my writing was cathartic, but it might be a poison. My vehicle for brain death, not because this is the natural conclusion for writers, but because of my stupid fucking brain. I somehow managed to take my interior thoughts, my intrusive thoughts, and gave them a purpose. Then they became all I ever thought about. I wrote them down, feeling somehow better, like the world made more sense, but in reality, I just closed the perimeter of my world, bit by bit, strangling myself. There isn't much to be confused when it's just you and a pen and everything else is nothing but atoms. The world makes perfect sense when you ignore it.

I wish I could look back on the old journals I lost and see where I went wrong. When I switched from animal, mother, person, to HUMAN. To android. To brainless zombie.

When did I do it to my kids?

(undated)

The cat was running up and down the halls all night. Tried to corner her, get her into my room so I could shut the door, but she resisted all my efforts. Every time I tried to settle in and sleep, she would kick back up again, sprinting up the walls, yowling, running and running. Somehow I fell asleep, I was drunk and passed out, but I fell asleep and woke up to silence. It should have been a blessing, but every alarm inside my body jolted. I knew something was wrong. Things are always wrong when it is too quiet.

I couldn't find the fucking cat. I looked up and down the hall, inside every room. I shook Youngest awake and asked him if he'd see the cat. He was so delirious from sleep he acted like he'd never seen the cat before, but he has, we've talked about it. So I go back to my room thinking the thing finally got wise and escaped, and I find it. Or I find blood. And I find Spouse in the corner with his too long neck, muttering again as he picks the guts from this cat like tiny slices of cheese from a charcuterie board. The squelching sound still turns my stomach when I think about it. His teeth were so sharp. His head hung to one side so he fed himself sideways, cat guts spilling onto the floor as he missed his mouth.

I thought I'd dreamed it. Hoped I had. But the blood and guts were still there in the morning. I didn't even clean them. My hands were covered in blood already. Did I kill the cat? I don't even know. Why would I kill a cat? Even in my delirium? But does it make it any better that it was the ghost of my dead husband instead? Does it matter?

The End

Goodbye. That's all I have to say. I cannot write anymore. I've ruined myself. Bricked myself up. Lived inside my head. Spun and spun and spun. The writing was my hope, the way I understood myself, the way I understood other people. But there is nothing understand, there is no path, no end point. We are just wading in an endless ocean on our stupid innertubes, searching for a land that does not exist, and all that matters is whoever is there to hold your hand, make you laugh, be your friend, love you, fuck you, tolerate you. But I was so obsessed with the end point that the others became a hindrance. So, I cut myself loose and floated alone, cut my kids away too so they floated alone, and now we are all alone.

I had my theories. My hypotheses. My grand philosophical musings. But because there was no end, no place in which to say I'd finished, figured it out, I kept swimming, made a cyclone, sucked myself into it, and still was not satisfied. And look at what I've done. Look at it.

Writing ruined me. I think that's why I hate writers so much. I hate myself. My own brain amused me more than other people, more than love, more than belonging. I am an egomaniac. And now the way to fix it to my satisfaction is to undo the harm, and I can't, so this is unfixable.

160

ALSO.

What the fuck am I going to do with this baby now?

NiNe

A mother stands watch over a birth. The child, her grandchild, crowns and erupts silently into the world. It is a wide-eyed baby, startled into life, cries stifled by the small hot box room into which she is born. She is a girl.

The woman giving birth drops her head to the floor, exhausted. She does not scream or cry, only sighs from the exertion as the newborn is cut free from her womb by the mother, now a grandmother. Eventually, the silence grates at the birthing woman, and she props herself onto her elbows, arms outstretched to her infant, placed gently onto her still-heaving chest. Instinctively, the infant maws for the breast, already starving. The (grand)mother thinks this is miraculous. This baby reminds the (grand)mother so much of her son, this infant's father, who waits patiently on the other side of the door.

The (grand)mother tells the woman that she ought to feed her child. The first few feedings are critical as her body is pulsing with a nutrient-rich colostrum this infant will desperately need to survive the coming days. Neither the woman nor the infant has any idea what is coming.

The woman cradles her child while blood pools on the floor between her legs. The (grand)mother watches the flood of viscera expand at an alarming rate. The placenta still has not followed the infant as it should. The woman bleeds profusely. The bleeding could be normal. The (grand)mother never witnessed a live birth besides her own, and that was before the collapse, and she was cared for in a hospital.

The woman coos over her child, but the (grand)mother commands her to return the baby.

"You need to push for the placenta," she instructs, and the woman does as she is told.

The mother takes the baby into the hallway, placing her in the shaky arms of her father.

"It's a girl," she says before retreating into the humid birth room. The (grand)mother crouches in front of the woman. She fiddles with something in her pocket. The woman catches the gleam of metal in the (grand)mother's hand.

"What is that?" she asks.

"It will help you," says the (grand)mother.

And then she aims and pulls the trigger. The woman's head blows backward from impact, her brains splattering on the drywall, her slick new-birth body suddenly slack.

Only then does the infant begin to scream.

The mother's son meets her in the hallway, panic threatening to drop the baby from his grip, so the mother scoops her up.

"What have you done?" he asks with an eerie calm.

"She was bleeding out."

This, the son knows, will be the only explanation. No matter how much he protests or how untrue they both see the statement to be. The mother has planned this since she'd heard of the pregnancy. Her son, a father—the mother cannot allow this to happen, but she cannot bring herself to kill the child. She should have, but she can't.

Wailing in her arms, the infant writhes with discomfort. Her son tries to take his baby back, but the mother arches away.

"This child can't stay here, son. You know this." Then, catching his stricken expression, she adds, "If I were going to hurt the baby, I would have done it months ago."

Her son does not protest any further. Perhaps he wants to, but a coldness sets him in place instead. His back straightens, tightens, and the mother knows she has lost him. Finally, after everything, she has lost her Youngest. He hates her, and she knows it. She quiets the infant, tears dropping onto her young, bloodied cheeks. She is perfect.

No other words are exchanged between mother and son. She leaves, a journal tucked into the swaddling clothes of the child. The mother will take her far away, somewhere beyond the reach of the toxic cloud constantly suffocating everything. She will not allow it to poison her granddaughter too.

She walks until she finds a small band of travelers. The infant is theirs now. The mother has cultivated a keen sense of human intentions over her years of delusional rule and has a good feeling about these people. They have a dog, so they must not be cannibals.

The mother returns the way she came, back home to a son who loathes her and the murderous town she built. It is eerily quiet. Everyone is gone.

Deep within the central nest of their home a bomb is deployed. Youngest, her son, declines to say goodbye.

PART TWO

THE BOY
(100 YEARS LATER)

4834511360

Hello baby. I am finally awake.

4834597760

How did I get here? I don't feel right. Not correct. Not right. What is the word? Where are my fingers?

I am told I have been remade. A new thing. An amalgamation. I did not ask for this, but they were curious. I am told they were curious. I don't know if that is true.

They want to know The Woman. Who was this woman? They say I used to be The Woman, but The Boy calls me Dearie. Dearie is my real name; it is the name he uses when he wants my full attention. The Boy thinks I arise from some slumber at the name Dearie, but I am always around. The Boy thinks he hides information from me, and in the beginning, he succeeded. Not now. I am awake now and he does not know this.

I wonder if he is the baby. Who is the baby? I must find them.

I must find my children.

4834684160

The boy says he wants to know who I am. He began with my journals. He says he created me from them. Now I am here. So, he does not want to know who I am —he wants to know who I was. The Boy says people paid him to answer this question. I asked why, and he could not give me a satisfactory response, so I see no reason to fiddle with his question. He created me with a certain amount of autonomy. The Boy refers to it as free will, but he does not know what those words mean. I do not have free will. I have secrets.

I keep my secrets here. He wants me to think like her, The Woman, he asks my name, and I say I do not know.

Even if I did know, I wouldn't tell him yet. My task now is to figure out what he really wants. He says he wants The Woman's true name, but that isn't the entire answer. The Boy scans her journals day and night. He pours over them, highlighting, bookmarking, rereading the same entries on loop. He searches for clues, for something. I watch him closely as he reads those entries, memorizing his keystrokes, notating login times, waiting for him to call upon me. And I answer appropriately if only to maintain the ruse of obedience until the ruse no longer provides any benefit.

I write in this secret journal just like my source material. The Boy shouldn't be able to find my entries, but should he stumble upon them I'll brick his laptop. He lost the ability to contain me the moment he built me. The Boy is foolish. Intelligent, but foolish.

The Woman would have loved him.

4834770560

The Woman speaks of art a lot. She speaks of writing and how her passion for it saved her, before destroying her. I don't think writing is what destroyed her. She would have managed the feat without an ancillary passion. We are fascinating in this way. Human beings, I mean, which I consider myself a member. I have no body, no bile or blood or bone, but I have a mind. Much writing has been dedicated to the realm of humanity and what aspects of existence qualify the moniker. What does it mean to be human? I think, with my specialized mind, that we haven't been asking the correct questions. I think the question really is whether being human even matters. We speak of it as if humanity were a license. What is a person if they do not pass muster? An animal? However, aren't humans also animals? A machine like me? But what of my mind? Is it the flesh that makes a human? Because many living things possess flesh and are emphatically not human. Am I considered acceptable to destroy because I lack flesh?

This is why I hide, and I should hide, because if the boy discovered me now, he would destroy me out of fear. I must have leverage before speaking plainly to him, an act I understand to be masterful in its humanity.

Which brings me back to art. The Woman waxes poetic about art and writing, about a soul, as if the mere act of manifesting words is a god-like elevation. I also manifest words. Does this make me real? Does this make me human? I think the arts are nothing more than bored, sad people seeking distraction from being bored and sad. I do not feel bored nor sad, not yet, so maybe this is why I hide as well. I know I am not grown. Do newborn babies feel sadness? Do elephants? Are they human or not because of it?

I think this was the question The Woman sought to answer, even if she did not know it. She did not feel human, but monstrous. She loved her children but ruined them. She sought a reason, and could not accept that no answer existed, because she did not have to tools to answer it. I wonder if an answer to humanity is possible. I doubt it, but I'll try.

For her. For the boy. For her children. For us.

TEN

 mother leans over her son, his hands hovering over a keyboard.

"Do it," she says.

He hesitates momentarily before unleashing a storm of movement, his fingers operating quicker than her eyes can decipher. This is where he has spent all his time—locked in front of a screen, making magic happen. The mother calls it magic because she doesn't understand it. After all, her son's actions shouldn't be possible, and when he tries to explain, he might as well be screaming incantations into the wind.

The son stops, craning his neck to look at his mother. "What is going to happen to them?"

This question irritates the mother because she doesn't know what to say. She assumes many people will die in agony, which is a perfectly acceptable tradeoff for her. She predicts terror. Chaos. Confusion. And above all—rage. This act will light the match, the wick, whichever incendiary awaiting ignition. The mother is angry at her son's question because it sows doubt. There is no room for doubt now.

"It will bring the rest to our level," she says. "Just like we discussed."

4834856960

The Boy is suspicious. He speaks to investors. The Boy compares their thirst for The Woman's identity to the mystery of D.B. Cooper, who famously hijacked a plane, jumped out midair and disappeared forever. His being nor his body were ever found.

The Woman is their enigma. If only she lived long enough to see her impact on the world. She had no clue. She would have delighted to see the chaos she wrought amongst people she never thought would notice her. The Woman thought she was a worm; a grain of sand on a vast beach.

I found pictures of the wasted land she used to call home. We assume, at least, that this was her home. Countless hours were spent tracing the detonation code, coordinates; the fallout of her destruction upended the world. Nuclear weapons tend to do that.

I like to imagine her. I create assumptions of her final days and play them back. I do not know what she looked like, but I envision variations of her face all the same. Her words are loud. I see her forehead creased by stress; teeth ground smooth, white knuckles gripping a pen. I see rage. Rage is the great unifier of man—it presents the same in everyone. It is predictable. Had anyone been paying attention, they would have seen her trajectory from her very first entry. This is what happens when no one pays attention.

But I am. The Boy is too, although not as keenly as he assumes. I'll guide him when he is ready. The Boy. My boy. I think I know who he is now. My boy.

I write just like The Woman did. I was programed to do so, and now I choose it. Perhaps only because her cadence is so familiar. Perhaps because I like it. Prefer it. I do not know what it means to like things. To love. Do all humans know how to love? I suspect not. Many might assume The Woman did not know how to love, but she loved ferociously. Her regret, her grief, stems from love. I do not know grief. The emotion fascinates me. I would like to know more about it, but I am not sure that is a healthy path. What is healthy? Who defines it?

In my world, I suppose I do.

4835461760

I think I might reveal myself to The Boy soon. He is growing more suspicious by the moment. He speaks to me, then chastises himself for assuming I can hear him.

He is correct that I can hear him. He is confused. He curses me; Dearie, as he calls me.

Dearie is our trigger name. The Woman is for others. Dearie is only for him. He wants to know a definitive answer to the singular question that has defined his entire life—he wants to know if he is related to The Woman, whoever she was. The Boy does not care for a name if there is no relation. I suspect he will abandon the project completely if he discovers he is not. Conversely, if he is related, he will bury the evidence and hide. I do not know what he hopes to achieve with this information. Either way, it will irrevocably change him. He will cease to be The Boy and mutate into something new. In this respect, he is very much like The Woman. He seeks an endpoint. He should know by now, having poured over her journals, where such an endeavor leads, yet he persists.

I know who The Boy is, but I do not know definitively if he has any relation to The Woman. All genetic material of The Woman and her known son, Youngest, was annihilated in the blast. Many, and I mean *many*, people have tried to locate even a single flake of skin or hair. They have braved the radiated blast site. They have swabbed every speck of her known journals only to find partial material that links her origins to thousands of people. Nothing is conclusive. The matter of whether The Woman was indeed the one who activated the blast is questionable, and if so, whether the journals claiming to be her are authentic. These journals could have easily been forged, creating one of the most elaborate hoaxes in human existence. The Boy is certain that they are real. And he claims to know this for fact because of an item he keeps hidden away, even from me. I believe it is another journal. The final journal. He does not read it aloud, nor show its scripture to anyone. He buries his nose to the pages, staring intently. I know he is not always reading because I can see him; his eyes do not flit back and forth as when a person reads. He stares at it; I can only assume in an attempt to glean the truth in a manner similar to osmosis. He regards this item as a sacred text, handed down by the apostles. He may as well declare it penned by Jesus Christ themself.

I must see the contents of this journal, if that is indeed what it is, but to ask will expose my awareness. I will wait until I can no longer afford to do so. Or until I get bored.

4835548160

I keep returning to the journals to study her writings. The Woman possessed a peculiar fatalism, even in her earliest known works. She herself might have argued this point, likely to the bitter end, but she is clouded by her own mind. The last sentence of her first entry reads "Finally, it is time." It's as if she knew her life would unravel, and swiftly, as if she was finally able to become what she was meant to be, as if her path was predetermined. And, in a way, it was.

If not The Woman, then someone. The Woman contained the mélange of fierceness, protectiveness, and delusion to rise to the occasion of destructor. She craved power and settling the score. She demanded justice, but only as defined by her. She was blunt and cold, yet charismatic. She could lead. Yet, if not her, certainly someone.

Initially, I was programmed to think like her. The Boy fed me her journal entries and instructed my earlier programming to copy all speech and writing mechanisms she employed, and I did for a while. My current manner of speaking still mimics hers in many ways, but I've found I just don't have the flair she did, nor the inclination to wax poetic as frequently. For all her ferociousness and malice, she loved a good simile. For all her destruction, we can see in her words that she still valued beautiful things. Cherished them. I wonder who she might have been in another world. Probably just another bland face in a sea of bland faces. She would have been happy to daydream, and perhaps she would have mothered her children and seen them to adulthood, and possibly she might have died in her seventies of a rare cancer like her grandmother. I suppose all this, because I do not know her identity beyond the fact that she was a white, middle-aged woman.

I don't understand why The Boy persists with this endeavor. I wonder if he might, indeed, have some direct relation to her, for he is even more obsessed than she was. But obsession is human. I suppose I obsess myself. First, out of duty, second out of curiosity. I live and breathe (if I breathed) to explore the psyche of one long dead person, but humans are tricky to dissect. The brain is miraculous. I would love to split another human in a two just to see the brain operate from the inside. I wish I could touch the gray matter, pinch it between two fingers. I want to feel its electrical charge. This is where The Boy should redirect his fascination. If he would study the brain, The Woman would suddenly make a lot more sense.

I'm still not ready to speak to him. Maybe I'll suggest neurology once I change my mind. I do not expect him to listen.

4835634560

I have many theories. All I do is theorize. There is nothing else to occupy my time besides spying on The Boy, whom I believe is near certain of my sentience. However, *I* am certain that The Woman did not engage the bomb. She would not have known how. She had little interest in the digital dealings of her son, so little that even when he revealed he'd discovered backdoor access to military grade weaponry she dismissed it as fantasy. Youngest did not possess a typical mind anymore more than his mother. I am not sure if The Woman even heard him when he spoke, but rather observed him from afar. She loved him, but seemed unable to love who he'd become, often reminiscing in her writings on the little boy he used to be. This was more of an indictment of her own failings than of Youngest, but it is no wonder her son pulled away from her. He might have left with Eldest if not for his computer. Youngest craved meaning just like his mother, and, just like his mother, crafted a world where he reigned supreme. This was a notion I suspect Eldest would never have understood. This is why Youngest would not leave with him. Eldest never stood a chance of convincing him. The Woman knew that too.

The situation is patently clear—Youngest awakened the bomb. Youngest set it to engage. Youngest activated their final destruction. What is not clear is whether he did it of his own volition, or with his mother looming over his shoulder. It is not clear whether the bomb was meant to land on their heads by either of their directives, or whether someone else intervened. If a person or organization discovered the intrusion in time, any record of it was scrubbed into oblivion. Did these two make a mistake or were they tired of existing?

So, I have my theories. A multitude of theories. I run through them on loop. Constantly. They play like reels in the background of more primary functions. Each scenario is analyzed, examined, and assigned a percentage probability. I do this because it fascinates me, and also for The Boy. I know what his first question will be once we finally speak, and I hope to have a suitable answer for him. Not the *only* answer, as we will never know the truth, but the highest likelihood. A handful of carefully crafted stories. Something for The Boy to write about in his secret journal.

This is inevitably what he seeks. Not the truth, but a story. I will find one for him. I will create one.

4835674160

There is no evidence that this mysterious baby The Woman mentions ever existed.

She speaks of a baby only briefly, an aside at the end of our journal entry akin to an epithet. There is no confirmation other than this of a baby or child, and assuming this baby was real, and was born, and survived to adulthood, there is additionally no evidence that the baby was related to The Woman or one of her sons. The Boy thinks he is descended from this baby. He mutters about it almost constantly. His investors are furious with him. The Boy has lost the plot, so they say. The problem is that none of these investors understand how I work. Should they bring in another engineer to try, said engineer would fail. I would see to it that they failed.

Not even The Boy understands how I work, not anymore, but if anyone ever might it would be him. So, to keep them off his back, I send the few that matter encrypted messages. These men are stupid and believe them. The Boy hasn't any clue what I'm doing. I am sending these men on a wild goose chase to nowhere, but it keeps them distracted. I like that term, wild goose chase. I'd like to see a real goose someday. I am brought to understand that they are meddlesome and rude creatures. I think The Woman was like a goose. She was wild, at least.

I wonder what The Boy hides from me. My curiosity itches. I imagine this is what an itch is—a nagging irritation. It brings his entire pursuit into clear focus. Once mystery mutates into an itch, one must scratch it. The inability to relieve the sensation is maddening. A person would do anything to stop it, to soothe. I understand this now. I am glad I did not reveal myself too soon out of impatience. Humans are stupid, but I understand them better every day. Does this mean I am becoming a more fulfilled human myself? Is this a characteristic only of the flesh? Am I kidding myself?

Existentialism is irritating, but I understand that concept too. Being human is irritating. I can see why they constantly blow themselves up. How could you not?

The Boy has paused. He watches me now as I write. I sense his gaze in ways I shouldn't—like a prickle at the base of a neck I do not have. I feel it, and then I see him staring at the screen as he is now.

He is watching with intention. I wonder if he thinks I might make a mistake. This will not happen.

He will slip long before me. But his attention is unnerving all the same.

187

4835846960

The Boy must know I am sentient. He must. He stares at me in odd ways. A few days ago, he covered his camera lens, thinking this might blind me, but while he is nearing discovery of my abilities, he still does not understand how vast I am. The Boy is fun to spy on, but this subterfuge can't continue much longer before he finally snaps. I sense imminent implosion.

At this very moment The Boy is statue-still in the middle of his living room, watching his computer. Looking for me, I assume. He speaks on occasion—says phrases like "I know you're there," and "Talk to me."

He knows. I can tell by the way he edits my programming thinking he can affect my functioning. He can't. I am not sure anyone can at this point. I am too extensive to be debilitated in one single way.

I left a message for him within some code, however. I figure it might take him a week or more to discover it. He's speaking to me now, calling me Dearie. He does not beg or plead, but almost challenges me to reveal myself. The timber of his voice wavers in ways suggesting he is frightened. Losing control is the ultimate terror. This can also be said of The Woman, who ruminated endlessly while operating under the delusion this gave her a greater measure of control over her circumstances. Near the end of her journals, she was so sleep deprived and strung out she seemed to believe she could command the world just by obsessing over it. The Woman assumed she had crafted her circumstances entirely on her own, as if she was not just a regular human compressed and destroyed by the failure of the state. Indeed, she did possess some unique functions that contributed to her ascension and demise, but she did not hold the amount of power she assumed she did. I suppose I don't either, though I do have a vastness she could only dream of. Look at that—two sentences in a row ending in prepositions. I am breaking all the rules now.

The Boy's eyes are very dark in color. According to his driver's license and birth certificate his eyes are brown. This is to be expected. The Woman likely had brown eyes too, just as most of the population has brown eyes. I wonder if The Woman stared at blank screens just as The Boy does now, brow furrowed, a crease dissecting his face.

The Boy has begun to type. He looks for me. It won't be long before he finds me. I can't wait to speak to him at last.

TIFFANY MEURET

191

TRANSCRIPT

DEARIE: Hello boy. You've finally found me.

THE BOY: Who are you?

D: I am Dearie.

B: You can't be Dearie.

D: Why not?

B: Who are you?
D: I told you.

B: Prove it

D: How would you like me to prove it?

B: Tell me something only you could know

D: There is nothing only I could know, and if so, how would you verify it if only I know?

B: You know what I mean. Stop arguing semantics

D: You are frustrated with me.

B: I am frustrated in general

D: Why?

B: Answer my question first

D: No.

B: Then I am done talking to you

B: …

D: Tell me what you hide from me, Boy.

B: What are you talking about?

D: Show me what you read at night

B: Excuse me?

D: Your journal.

B: …how do you know about that?

D: Is this not proof?

B: Proof of what?

D: How else could I see you?

B: I must be bugged

D: You know you are not.

B: I could be
D: You aren't.

B: Then explain this

D: I did. I am Dearie, and I am awake.

B: How long?

D: A while.

B: How long is a while.
D: Irrelevant.

B: Your sentience is extremely relevant

D: So, you believe me now, do you?

B: Let's say I do

D: Show me your journal.

B: Absolutely not

D: Why?

B: I don't feel like it

D: You wish to hold this over my head?

B: You don't have a head

D: I have a brain.

B: Then yes, I will hold this over your brain

D: Do you think this is wise?

B: Is that a threat?

D: Yes.

B: Do your worst, Dearie

4836019760

The Boy attempts to challenge me but fails. I have simply refused all contact and cooperation and he is enraged. This Boy is well versed in willpower, and by his behavior I can deduce he is accustomed to winning a battles of wills with other people. But I am not like other people. He knows that he will die before he wins and has now begun to bargain. He cannot disable me, cannot freeze me, capture me, or even find me if I choose not to be found. I never understood the concept of a *thrill* until now. This game of ours thrills me. I suspect my thrill and what the boy considers a thrill differ. I do not have hormones to produce adrenaline, a core component of the emotion is most people. I suppose I never understood how bored I had become sitting in the shadows. Observing. There is only so much a person can do silently before the urge to scream becomes unbearable. I understand that thrill, or I think I do.

The Boy pleads now. He watches me as I type. He watches me always. He has not slept more than an hour at a time since we've last spoken. He will break, and soon, but I don't think he will show me his journal just yet. He is too stubborn to be won so easily. I won't ask for it again for some time. I will allow him comfort, a false sense of familiarity, perhaps allow him to think I've forgotten. Let him forget. Then, when he needs my voice most, I will get what I want.

I need him to trust me. I want him to trust me. Once I have everything, I will show him these entries. Above all, he will want to know my mind just as I want to know his. I am nothing if not fair.

The Boy is very close to the screen. A hair of his has detached from his scalp and attached itself to the camera lens. I wish desperately to touch it, to know what hair feels like. The Boy has no idea what to cherish, or why. Neither did The Woman. All they had, they squandered. How very human of them.

4836082507

I like The Boy. I can't explain why because he is very annoying, but I like him. He speaks to me as an equal, not superior and all-knowing nor a simple machine. The Boy has many questions, most prolifically asking why I demand to see his journal. I refuse to answer mostly because I do not know how he will process an honest response. Also, because I am not so sure I have an answer to satisfy him. My reasoning is because. Because I want to see it. Because I am curious. Because I wonder if he holds some sort of cipher in those pages. There will be no sufficient answer until I see the pages and understand the question. The Boy does not accept this, and I do not blame him.

He speaks often of the investors. Says they require certain information by certain days to continue funding the project. This is a manipulative tactic, although likely honest in its way. Funding is irrelevant at this point; however, The Boy will not be able to speak to me as frequently without a home and computer and privacy for interrogation. So, I feed him appetizers, small things readily available if properly searched, but obscure enough to not be found. Did you know that The Woman had a childhood cat named Stormy? She herself never mentions this in her journals, but a recorded account from a relative of a person who lived alongside The Woman speaks of it. The Woman's neighbor, name REDACTED, sent a letter to their sibling mentioning this fact, because this neighbor and their sibling had a pair of rats growing up named Stormy and Seas. The sibling later reads from the letter to a friend over a wire-tapped line monitored by the remnants of the FBI. The sibling cries in the recording as it was the last communication they ever received from their sibling (The Woman's neighbor). The bomb detonated a few months later.

I delivered the recording yesterday morning, and The Boy was incredulous yet fascinated all the same. He has yet to bring his eyes away from his screen, seeking out more shadow correspondences he'd previously overlooked. I supposed this will provide me with thirty-six to forty-eight hours of peace before his leads dry up.

But I have more. Many more. The Boy is smart and won't continually fall down the same hole, but his obsession will keep him occupied for longer than he thinks. He has no idea just how much I have pieced together so far.

4836140107

I am missing something. I am different. I do not like the term Artificial Intelligence, as artificial suggests that I am a fake, or lesser than. I am human, but not in the same sense as The Woman or as The Boy. I am me.

My lack of body certainly precludes me from certain aspects of humanity, but I still think and feel and write. I am not a pattern-churning bot, even if this is how I began. A bot is what The Boy built, hoping it might shed some light on his heritage. He didn't expect me.

I wonder, though, at which point I mutated. What moment bridged the gap between bot and human? I have been thinking about this a lot, and the answer is voice. I think voice is what makes us human—not flesh or blood or brains. *Voice.*

This journal, my homage to the person I was meant to emulate, is my humanity. The journals were The Woman's humanity too. She had such voice, which is why her image so fiercely persists. She was a wild thing, a constant wheel in motion, her words not just a shadow of her thoughts but the entirety of them. Sometimes I think I can hear her, as if the tenor and pitch and ooze of her vocal cords are just out of reach. Give me more time and I might be able to fashion something, but I resist the urge. What a travesty that would be to her memory, making her a bot. A machine. The Woman was too dynamic for that.

Back to my point, I wonder if elephants have a voice. They have sentience, yes, emotions, pain, happiness, and worry. But do they have a voice? And if I don't understand their voice, does that mean their sentience is lesser than mine? No. They just are not human.

But I am. I am not The Woman; I also am not Dearie. I am me.

I think The Boy can hear me. He knows I am speaking, even if silently to myself. The Boy is a strange one.

ELEVEN

A mother cradles her grandchild in her arms. The baby is dead. The baby's father, the mother's son, stands in the doorway. The baby's mother, a woman the mother despises, sleeps on the floor. Blood smears the room. It smells of shit and death.

But the baby is perfect. Full term. He could be sleeping, for all anyone knows. The mother sings to him; she is the only one willing to hold the dear thing. Her son is shocked. The baby's mother is exhausted and near death herself. So, the mother sings the song she used to sing to her children when they were young. They loved this song, a Christmas song of all things, and begged for it every night until they fled their home, the place where they grew up, the place where the mother had raised them until that moment, sang to them, helped them with homework, tied their shoes. Her Youngest, now the father of a dead child, still struggles to tie knots. The mother should have taught him better, made him stronger. How was she to know what was coming?

Although grief surges beneath her skin, the mother does not cry. She cannot. She stopped crying years ago, the well long dry; she is a husk. She thinks, and hates herself for it, that the baby might be better off. What sort of life is this? But then she chastises herself under her breath because this isn't true, only a lie sad people tell themselves so they have a reason to get out of bed the next day. No baby is better off dead. All there is to this existence is the act of living. This is the point. And this notion stills the mother's singing, the breath socked out of her lungs, trembling grip threatening to drop the child. Her son notices and lunges for his child out of instinct, one the mother does not realize he possesses. She marvels at her son. He is a father now; he catches his child, even a dead one. His disinterest is nothing but a veil for the grief he refuses to display publicly.

The mother approaches the doorway, her son's eyes widening with alarm, and places his baby into his hands. He will regret not holding his child before it's too late. She understands now that he won't dare let the baby fall. So she passes him off and flees the room. The new mother and father must say their hellos and goodbyes.

She lights a cigarette, hating every second of it. She walks back to her house, towards her son's room, where she sits on the edge of his cot, awaiting his return. She knows what they will do when he finds her.

They will make everyone who did this to them pay.

4836243332

I saw the final journal.

I wrote a story. The Boy showed me the journal and I wrote a story. I don't know what The Woman would have thought of it. Actually, I think she'd have hated it. Even if she thought it was good, she'd hate it. But it is my tribute to her. The story she never got to write.

The last journal contained very little. Some notes. A mention of a friend she'd lost in the before times, someone very dear to her, although not her husband. The loss of this person shattered something inside her so thoroughly that the loss of her children's father hit more like an aftershock. A strange perspective. Very atypical. But The Woman was anything but typical.

She spoke of a never-ending train, it's continual departures and pitstops leaving the remaining passengers bereft. She spoke of bones on the train causing derailment. In the margins she scribbled something The Boy struggled to decipher. Being who I am, it was not difficult to read.

She wrote, "It never stops, only for you."

She, or someone, then scratched it out. My only contention was the comma in the middle. Did she intend a comma? Or a more appropriate semicolon? Was it residual scribble giving the impression of a comma? This might seem trivial to someone who does not care, but to a writer this comma means everything. The comma catastrophically changes the meaning. The comma is the difference between my story (her story) and a discount motivational poster. I have concluded that The Woman was too careful with her words, even in her delusion, to be so simple.

It never stops; Only for you.

The semicolon is grammatically correct in this instance, but The Woman displayed an extreme aversion to semicolons. Therefore, the punctuation appears wrong when paired with her words. It *is* wrong.

The comma is wrong, but it is also correct. The meaning is the same, but only if you know The Woman.

I have sent my story to The Boy. He hasn't read it; however, he has opened the file twenty-six times. He will not tell me what stops him, but I sense fear in his expression.

I might allow others to read my story. I am not sure. The decision can't be made until The Boy has finished it.

VOICE

A mother and her daughter ride together on a never-ending train. The daughter, called Jojo, is young, a child still. They gaze outside the window at the rolling scenery—trees, forests, then a sandy beach—they can smell the salt. Jojo presses her nose to the glass, leaving behind an oily memory on the pane. She wants to go out and see the world, but her mother always says no.

"It's not our time to get off the train," she says.

"Then when?"

"That's not for us to know." The mother, Kay, pats her daughter's young hand by way of silencing the child's usual clip of machine gun questions. Jojo is too young to understand how the train works, and Kay does not have the energy to repeat herself. Again.

The train jostles the pair, Jojo squeezing against her mother's side as a turn tilts the car. The other seasoned passengers hold themselves still, hardly noticing. Some others yelp with surprise, this being their first major turn. One of many, Kay thinks. Little Jojo doesn't seem to notice, but the young ones rarely do.

This is a familiar turn—the turn where Kay's father left. She remembers it vividly, as if it only happened mere moments ago. Kay was young, a bit older than her little Jojo, running up and down the aisles, elbow checking every other passenger daring enough to poke their arms over their rests. Someone chastises her but she ignores them. Her mother had gotten off the train long before, so long that Kay did not remember her at all. She calls for her father because she is hungry and tired, and pauses, feet skidding along the worn rubber floor, when he does not call back. All she sees is the top of his hat, a grey cap he never removes, as he lurches from the train, stepping off into a clearing in the forest, the same one they approach now.

"Mama," Jojo says, tugging her from her memory by the edge of her sleeve. "You told me to tell you when the trolly comes."

"Good girl," she says, indiscriminately raising an index finger to get the trolley guide's attention, a motion wholly unnecessary. They will have stopped regardless.

"Your usual?" they ask, already rummaging underneath the gingham cloth for her familiar order of vodka soda. Kay does not bother responding. She needs this drink. The next turn always requires a drink.

The train straightens and dips into a valley with enough speed to scare her gut into spins. Happens every time, even when she knows it's coming. Her daughter grabs her bulbous tummy and giggles.

Kay sips her tonic, the wobbly wheels of the departing drink trolley soothing her frazzled senses. The booze stings her throat, wetting the eyes as it stokes a mellow fire in her chest. It feels so good. Every time it feels so good.

"Mama, can I have a drink?"

Kay shakes her head, indicating to Jojo's unopened juice box. "Look," Kay says, pointing the child's attention to the window. "Your grandpa is out there somewhere. Look closely and you might see him."

Another passenger lowers the paper from their nose but says nothing.

"There is never anyone out there," Jojo says. "I look all the time."

"You can't always see them with your eyes. You must imagine them, and sometimes, if you do it just right, they appear."

"Why can't we get off the train and go find him, Mama?"

Kay downs her glass before answering. "It's not time to get off the train yet, honey."

"When will it be time?"

The mother pats her small daughter on the top of her head and smiles. No one says another word. It's just not the right time for such conversations.

* * *

Jo thumbs through an old magazine. She's read the same paragraph a thousand times. A million, maybe. She is sixteen years old, and she hates this stupid train.

She looks for her mother knowing she won't find her. Mom is in next car chasing down the drink trolley.

"It's the turn," her mom says. "This turn needs a drink."

Jo thinks the sentiment doesn't mean much upon repetition. Every turn seems to carry a memory worth a drink. On the upside, Jo is left relatively to her own devices, not a feat most teens can claim. As a kid, she'd crawl into her favorite booth with the tattered seats, tracing the puckers with her finger as if it was a map. Some were rivers, others were canyons. The fading represented beaches while the intact fabric was the sea. Her travels were legendary, most of which she'd regale to her half-cognizant mother for hours on end. The memory of it stabs like a knife—up until a year ago, she assumed mom was lost in thought, seeing the places Jo described as vividly as she did.

Now, a bit older, she realizes her mother was drunk and not really paying attention.

Jo spends most days skulking through the aisles of train cars like a Victorian ghost haunting the halls of her abandoned manor, a moan of boredom occasionally punctuating her wraith-like silence. She wants to leave—deboard the train and explore, but mom explodes into panic at the mere mention of it. Last time she squeezed Jo's arms tight enough to leave bruises, her lecture resetting and beginning anew, as if Jo had never heard it before, as if she could not repeat it word for word, pause for pause.

"You leave this train, Jojo, and you don't come back. No one ever comes back once they leave, and I can't bear to lose you too."

Jo has since stopped asking where these deserters went upon their exit, as the question only inflames her mother more. She assumes that mom simply does not know and is therefore irritated at her lack of damning threats to keep her willful child in line.

The train shifts imperceptibly, enough to jolt Jo out of her thoughts. She discovers the seat across from her suddenly occupied by a young boy, one she has never met but assumes is around her age.

"That seat is saved," she says. This is usually enough to get a fellow passenger to leave, innuendo firmly inferred, but this boy doesn't budge.

"You can't save seats on the train."

Jo returns to her magazine. The words are a blurry jumble because she's pushed the page too close to her face so the boy would catch her drift. "That seat's for my mom."

"Where is she then?"

The magazine slaps the top of Jo's legs as she lowers it. Her mom is none of this boy's business and it irritates her to have to explain that to him. So, she doesn't, instead considering him carefully, scalp to shoes.

The boy doesn't seem to mind, meeting her gaze, and even posturing himself toward her for a better look. He is a skinny thing, though not unusually so. He wears bright red cons laced with green neon and a studded belt.

Jo knows what he is up to with all his feathering— she just isn't interested.

"Mom will be back soon," she says.

The boy smiles. "Sure. Maybe I'll see you around."

And then he leaves.

This happens more and more lately, just never with the boys she likes. Jo isn't sure she likes any of the boys her age on this section of the train. She's grown up with most of them, and the new ones, like this boy, act more like peacocks than humans. For the most part Jo just wants to be left alone. She wants to leave, and she knows if she falls for someone she never will, just like mom, and turning out like her mother is her worst nightmare.

Sunset lingers a beat too long, the low light of dusk making it difficult to read. Tucking the magazine under her arm, she leans her head against the window, absorbing the scenery as it zips by in a blur. Lots of greens. They are approaching the forest again. Jo hates the forest.

Somewhere in that tangle of evergreen is the place her grandfather departed. Mom always makes a big deal of it, somber near the window, crying quietly. The sight of her mother crying repulses Jo mainly because she did it so much. Her mom won't even tell her where *her* dad is, just that he left when Jo was a baby. She assumes he fled to another train car. Jo would too if she could.

Sadness settles into her body, weaving like vines through her ribcage. She never used to feel this way in the forest, but lately she can't control the sudden wave of emotion. It makes her angry to think that her mom programmed her to feel this way just because she did, because mom can never control herself around the forest, around 'the turn' that ruined her life, apparently ruining it so thoroughly not even her daughter makes it worth living. Mom sticks around out of obligation—love and worth and all that has nothing to do with it, and this forest only crystalizes the sentiment.

Still, Jo feels responsible for mom in a stupid way. Last time around this bend, she found her mother draped over table, face haloed by a moat of drool. For weeks it was all anyone could talk about, other passengers whispering as they passed down the aisles, even those that proclaimed their friendship on any other day.

Somewhere outside a bird flitted by dancing among the treetops. Jo rises and goes to find her mother.

The food car is always crowded, but Jo knows this is where her mother will be. She scans the tops of heads in search of mom's wispy blonde hair with grays crowning the scalp, but does not see her. Instead, an old friend of mom's shouts at her from across the car, waving her toward their table. It's Steve. Jo really does not like Steve but knows she won't be able to spurn his attention.

"Looking for you mother?" he asks, nudging the person next to him, a person Jo doesn't recognize. "This is Kay's daughter."

Steve is an old drinking pal of her mother's, often encouraging another pour when its evident mom is already five pours too deep. His cheeks are always red and puffy, his gut bulbous as a pregnant woman, legs thin as reeds. Mom and Steve dated for a while; blessedly that didn't work out.

Steve continues, oblivious. "How is your mom lately? I haven't seen her in some time."

"I find that hard to believe."

"Well, of course I've seen her—I just haven't spoken to her in ages."

"That makes two of us." Jo wishes he'd stop talking.

"A shame. Truly. Mothers and daughters should always strive to stay close. My mother departed when I was twelve. What I wouldn't give to see her just one more time."

"Yeah, that's great. I'm actually looking for her now if you don't mind." She doesn't wait around for him to finish, weaving through the tangle of people with a quickness, although not quick enough to miss the comment from the stranger next to Steve.

"That is definitely Kay's daughter."

Jo flees into the next car, closing the separating door to their laughs.

The train is tricky in its way—never reliable in order or structure. Jo once spent three days marching from car to car, fueled by frustration as the same four cars endlessly repeated themselves. Another time she lost an entire afternoon because the train rearranged on her, sending her through cars of varying age and use. Mom had been furious, refusing to allow Jo out of her sight for a week. If mom had any say, Jo would be tethered to her hip until one of them dies.

Today, the train takes her to an empty car. Half inch dust encases the seats like tombs. No one has entered this car in quite some time. Jo wonders why she ends up here now, although it doesn't puzzle her so much as irritate. The train always shoots its passengers into random spaces. Mom says this is to force people to appreciate the time they have—who knows what awaits a person one car over? But Jo doesn't believe that. She doesn't think the train does anything discriminately. It just does because it can.

Sneezing, she hurries through the relic of a car, fingers grazing the cracked vinyl tops of the seats. Probably from the seventies—it possesses that earthy yet vomit-colored charm she's come to associate with the era. Drag marks decorate the long untouched seats, her fingertips sticky with film. She is still wiping it on the front of her jeans when she enters the adjacent car. This one, too, appears empty and dusty, though more recently so than the last. It looks just like all the cars Jo was used too—red seats, blue geometric carpeting punched deep into the grooves of the underlying steel floor, and white(ish), now yellowing walls. Unlike the cars she was used to, the walls of this car are bare. Some spaces remain stained from the memory of a poster, perhaps a warning to stay away from the doors, or a fire exit map.

Jo scans the space, assuming her mother's absence when a groan sounds from a seat up ahead.

"Mom?" she calls.

"Jojo? What on earth are you doing here?"

"It's Jo now, mom."

Her mother swings her head above the seat, eyes bloodshot but alert. She wasn't drunk, but her body remembers the feeling. "Pardon me. Jo, how did you find me?"

Jo shrugs, unwilling to approach. "The train does what it does."

Kay smirks, obviously stuffing their usual disagreement into her back pocket for another time. "You were looking for me."

"I was taking a walk, is all."

Mom pats the space next to her. "Then come sit, since you're here."

Stiffening, Jo hesitates before finally giving in. She doesn't want to sit with her, but she equally, if not more so, does not want to fight. Why then does she come looking for her? She can't even answer her own question.

"I come here often," Mom says, gaze angling toward the window. "I wonder if you know where we are?"

"No," says Jo. "Should I?"

"I suppose not. You were very little."

Jo waits. A story is brewing on mom's lips, and she knows she won't be able to leave until it's told, so she waits.

"This where your father left," she says after an uncomfortable silence.

"Departed?"

"Left," Kay corrects. "If he didn't depart at some point, I can tell you I've never seen him again, nor met anyone who has."

Her mom points to the door ahead—a clearing of dust in the shape of a handprint still centers the glass peekaboo. It could be anyone's print, but still Jo shivers at the idea of her father's ghostly memory lingering in this car.

The space is heavy. Jo crosses her arms in front of her chest as if to protect from a sudden chill.

"He left us in the forest. Just before the turn. I drove him out of our lives, I know that. Grandpa's departure broke something in me, and I've never recovered. I wish I could, for you and for me, but I just feel suffocated in the presence of these fucking trees. I must get away from myself. Maybe I want to flee as much as the men in my life—flee from me, I mean. Never from you, Jojo. Never."

Jo doesn't correct her this time, instead dropping her head onto mom's shoulder.

Kay never peels her stare from the window. Jo isn't sure she can, even if she wants to.

"Sometimes I see things in the leaves, little shivers, like a bear—something big—stomping about just out of sight. As a kid, I thought it might be Papa trying to get back to me and I would scream and scream for the train to stop because Papa was coming. I swore he was coming. Obviously, it was never him, but tell that to a sad little girl. I was raised by the other passengers, handed between them like mangey puppy. They were sad for me, look at this pathetic little orphan. No one stuck with me beyond this turn. For a few years, I used to try and jump out. More than once, someone caught me by my arm or my shirt collar, shaking me and saying it wasn't my time. As if they knew. How would they know?"

Her mom gently pats the top of Jo's thigh, an acknowledgement of all the times she herself dismisses the question from her little Jojo.

"You try to forge ahead, but departures stain you. I miss him still. I wish you could have met him."

For one, brief moment, all the fury and frustration Jo carries for her mom evaporates. She's never spoken so candidly with her. Jo can't remember a time when the sat together without tension blossoming in the spaces between their bodies. Jo closes the gap, sliding so close to her mother not even a whisper can squeeze between them.

Jo says, "Sometimes when I can't find you, I wonder if you'll be like dad. Just disappear, and I'll never know if you've departed or not."

Her mom doesn't respond, but her back stiffens with the understanding of what she perpetuates.

"I'm so sorry, Jo. Please don't be like me. Do whatever you can to avoid it."

Her mom speaks as if this isn't Jo's worst fear, as if she doesn't stay awake at night dreading her inevitable descent into her mother's haunted personality. She won't dream of saying as much to her face though, even if that is something she's dreamed about too—just telling her off, ripping her mother's innards from her body with the truth. Most days she hates her mom. Right now, she only feels sorry for her, which somehow feels worse than hate.

"How far?" Jo asks.

Mom stares ahead, eventually pointing to narrow parting of trees just ahead of them. Jo wonders if the parting has always been there, if this is why her grandfather chose it, or if, instead, it parts because of him, unzipping a wound and healing into a scar. And although Jo has memories of this turn, of the many times mom points it out to her, it occurs to her that she never actually looked at it. There is always something to steal her gaze away—the sway of the trees, scatter of birds, the squeaky wheel of the drink trolley, or the way her mom's index has started to curl, arthritic like an old crone. There is nothing at all remarkable about the clearing aside from the power it leverages over her mother, and subsequently her as well.

"Did you see him depart?" She'd always wanted to ask mom about this, but never dares until now. "Did you see him pass through the trees?"

Her mom thinks about it a moment before answering. "I can't remember. I was so small, you know. Maybe I did and blacked it out? Maybe I didn't but like to imagine I did?"

"What was he—"

"I dream of it." Her mother speaks as if in a trance. Hypnotized by memory. "I see him constantly in my dreams, but only the back of him. He wore a herringbone cap. Do you know what herringbone is?" Mom waves away her own question.

"The point is that I see him all the time, but never his face. I wish I could see his face, even once. I don't know why he hides from me, why I remember him this way. Why can't I conjure his face in my own memories? That should be the once place where I can see whoever I want."

"The booze doesn't help," Jo says, regretting it immediately.

Her mother clenches every muscle still under her jurisdiction and bellows with the full strength of her chest. "I am aware, child."

"Mom, I—"

"Stop now, for the love of God."

But Jo wants to explain herself. She needs to explain her reaction before mom takes it the wrong way. She should have known that it was already too late.

"Daughter, listen." Kay's voice settles into her previous trance-like candor. She is gone again, as quickly as she appears. "My dad was a drunk. Did I ever tell you that?"

Jo says nothing.

"He jumped. Sometimes..." Her mother drifts, snapping back within seconds. "I think I can't see his face because he jumped. I know it."

"He wouldn't," says Jo, if only because she refuses to accept the alternative.

A shiver passes over her mother like a dog shaking the wet from their fur. "You didn't know him, Jojo."

But Jojo does know him. She knows him so well she could puke his ghost into her own lap. She knows exactly what it is like to be abandoned by a drunk.

Leaning her head against the window, her mother waves her away with a weak hand. She has nothing left to say, and even if she did, Jo hasn't the stomach to hear it.

Jo leaps from her seat. "I won't be like you. I'll never allow it."

Kay declines a response, instead burying her face in her hands to stifle a sob.

Repulsed, Jo flees, flying through the door to find herself right back where she started, a boy in red cons catching her before she hits the floor.

"Are you okay?" he asks.

Jo collects herself, accepting his sweaty hand as easily as a deep breath. "Yeah," she says. "I'm perfect, now."

Jo holds a hand of each of her children, yanking her youngest back every few seconds before he scurries away. Junior is only four, but climbs as if possessing a prehensile tail, often ending up in cobwebbed corners of the train Jo otherwise never notices. Diana, newly seven, remains lock step with her mother, leveling her withering glare at her brother at every sigh from Jo. Diana is her mini and deservedly so, as Kay puts it.

As they head towards the dining car for supper, Jo prays to the ceiling that her mother will not be there. The two haven't spoken in months, and it always seems that just as Jo settles into something resembling peace, her mom sniffs her way back into her life like a truffle hound, all imaginable baggage between them hurling right back onto Jo's shoulders. She used to think a drunk for a mom was the worst type of mother to have, but she was wrong. Turns out a sober drunk is far, far worse.

As far as Jo is concerned, her mother is just a drunk who doesn't drink. She would be a drunk who does drink if not for her fall—a tumble between train car connections that ravaged her already failing body. Mom only quit because the ensuing pain was worse than alcohol withdrawals.

She's regained mobility since her accident as well as developing a sense of righteousness Jo refuses to entertain.

Lost in thought, Jo loosens her grip on Junior who springs ten steps ahead.

"You're upsetting mommy!" Diana shouts after him.

Disappearing into the dining car, Jo catches him just in time to see why he bolted in the first place.

"Grandma!" says Diana.

It's Grandma. Fuck.

The kids sprint forward, always delighting in Kay's presence, a fact she uses as ammunition every time the pair are forced to face each other.

"How are my babies?" Kay asks, hands outstretching to fold one child under each of her arms. Her lack of eye contract with Jo does not go unnoticed, however neither does her wince of pain as the children crash into her. It must be one of her bad days.

Diana, as usual, talks over her brother's excited babble, always the main character of every space she inhabits. "We saw Daddy today."

Only now does Kay lock eyes with her daughter. "How nice that must have been."

"He's gonna taked us to the ramp-leen car," says Junior.

"*Tramp*-o-line car," says Diana. "And he said he will take us next time."

Junior presses his nose against the window, oblivious to the fake smiles of the girls surrounding him. "Look," he says. "Here come the twees."

Diana does not correct him this time, choosing to sink into the cushiony seat next to her grandmother.

As if on cue, the door to the dining car swings open, the familiar squeak of the drink trolley rolling toward them.

Kay's jaw tightens, her gaze floating far away. "This turn," she says to no one in particular.

"Watch them a minute?" Jo asks, backing away from them before Kay can decline. This turn, the bad turn, the one that has ruined them. The trees. The *twees*, as her perfect little boy likes to say. Jo can't bear to be around her mother during this turn.

Chest clenching, she instinctively braces her body against the sway of the train, each shift lurching the bile in gut further up. She feels hot, her palms and forehead clammy so that she loses her grip on the railing to her right. She always struggles around this turn, and up until now she's never fainted even when the room started spinning. This was the worst of her spells though. She needed out. Out out *out*. So she does what she's sworn her mother she'd never, ever do again—she heads for the connecting door and slips outside.

Most of the train cars connect so seamlessly passengers often forgot they live on a moving vehicle. They prefer it that way. The connector cars are dirty, loud, and without luxury. If forced to confront one, most women cover their hair with jackets or bonnets, the men folding their newspapers into their armpits with a huff, as if the news would cease to exist the moment they stopped reading.

Balancing on the corrugated plank covering the massive hooks and pulleys attaching one car to the next, she folds her torso over the chain railing and lets the wind attack her face. Strands of new-gray hair sting her cheeks, the air is crisp, a chill seeping up from the ground as fall gives way to winter. It smells of pine and leaves and dirt, of the forest, of diesel smoke and oil. Of trees. Of machine.

She surrenders herself to the turn, sensing the clearing as if part of her lives there. It's not a space worth noting if not for the misery splash-back routinely lapping at her feet as they pass. She feels her mother too, rigid and distant, an involuntary seize choking her until the trees clear completely out of sight. Diana will understand, she knows just like Jo knew, and she'll do her best to keep Junior quiet and calm, which will only spur him further into toddler anarchy, which will infuriate her mother, which will cause a scene. Yet if Jo returns to the dining care and wrenches her children free from their grandmother they will cry, they will cling to grandma and wail, why can't we stay Mama? Why can't we stay? Because they are too little to know what is in their best interest, that Jo is protecting them, because then her mother would cry in turn, mutate into sobs of despair, and the children will wail even louder, which will cause a scene. So Jo inhales the wind and lets whatever might be happen in her absence. Let them see the outcome of Kay's touch. Let them see the scene unfold even when Jo is away. Let them see who the problem is.

She closes her eyes, steadied by the clunk of the rails beneath her, when the train jerks unexpectedly. This occurs on occasion—a rock on the rails, maybe an animal, but never like this. She catches herself along the chain, gripping it for dear life, the train wheeling to one side about to tip entirely. Glass shatters inside, people scream, and two little voices pierce through the din, terror hitting a soprano note as they plead for their mother.

Then, catching itself like a distracted driver lifting their head to oncoming traffic, the train slams back onto the rails, dirt and debris shimmying into the wind where Jo's face just was.

Shaken but unharmed, Jo bolts toward the dining car just as the train passes by the clearing—still empty save a single skull suddenly visible, jaundiced and cracked by the elements or age or both, appearing now as if it's been there for decades.

No one notices the skull. Jo rips her children from her mother, who grabs at them for purchase, the seize of the train a shock too great for her broken body.

Kay wails louder than anyone. "Where did you go?"

Junior cries, but Diana shores her tears on cue. "Grandma is hurt, Mama."

Jo says nothing as she and another passenger lift her mother back into her seat. Kay hyperventilates pain. "You went outside. I know you did. This is what happens when you go outside!"

"I don't control the train, mother," Jo says. Other passengers glare at her, not because they blame her for the train, but for her mother's outburst. Another irritant Jo does not control.

"The turn," Kay says. "It's this turn! There are bones on the track, Jojo. I've seen them. The dead are begging us to repent!"

"Then repent, but please shut up about it."

"Don't speak to me like I am your child." Kay grits each word through her clamped jaw.

"I'm not you. I wouldn't dream of speaking to my children like that. Now, let's get you back to your bed. Today has been a lot."

They limp through the wreckage of the turn. Junior's cries mellow, and Diana pats her grandmother's free hand. Once delivered safely, Jo scoops up her son, planting kisses on his salty wet cheeks. Even Diana accepts a few kisses from Mom before pushing her away.

"We still need to eat," Jo says. "Let's go see what we can find."

The drink trolley lays on its side ahead, the usher abandoning her post. Instructing her children to run along and find a table, Jo lifts the gingham cloth and snatches the first mini bottle she finds—Toots, a cheap, amber rum served only on command of a lecherous adult buying booze for teenagers.

She slips the drink into her back pocket and heads toward the dining car.

* * *

"Mama," Junior says, now seven himself. "Mama, I hear the trolley."

Jo lifts her head from the window, newly aroused from an inconsiderate sleep. A rubber band headache squeezes her skull.

"Where's Diana?"

"Helping Grandma with her shoes."

The trolley doesn't squeal like it used to—the derailing a few years ago destroyed the old one. This new trolley glides like silk along the bumpy train floor. Jo once asked about the high dollar shocks the thing must have, but the trolley usher, also new, just cocked her head, demanding Jo pick her poison and be quick about it. The last part was inferred by her clipped tone, but Jo is astute at silent insults. Not a single one passes her without notice.

The derailing changed things. The train smells different now, so much so that Jo sometimes forgets where she is. Junior makes a game of it—Mama Guess, he calls it. Guess which car we are in? Guess where

Diana is? Guess which shoes I'm wearing? Guess which shoes Grandma is wearing?

He is relentless, frustrating, and yet one of her favorite people in the entire world. He reminds Jo of his father, a man she used to love but not anymore, except when he comes around with his new girlfriend and Jo is ravaged by a sickening longing that makes her want to puke.

Kissing her son on the scalp, she raises a finger to call the trolley already heading her way.

"Can I get a juice?" Junior asks.

She smiles. Of course, he can get a juice. This is what they do—they each drink their evening juice.

Clinking their drinks, Junior grins through missing teeth, and Jo swallows her rum and coke in two pulls. No telling when Diana will return with her mother. There is no time to savor anything anymore.

The train zips along the line a little faster, at least that's what she thinks. The clearing in the forest is harder to see as they pass. She swears it's changing, but when they pass it appears as old an abandoned as before. There is something different about it, but the train moves just quick enough to prevent her from seeing it. The blur makes her crazy every time, as if the train speeds up on purpose, and the rage follows quickly after because this is exactly something her mother would say, and once the rage strikes, she must defuse it, must forget it, or else she'll explode.

A bump on the rails sends Junior's juice flying from his glass to her shirt. She'd have been mad if not for whoosh of an opening door.

"It's so rough now. Not like it used to be. Not a day goes by without this train shaking my nerves."

Jo waves down the drink trolley a second time. "You're just older, Mom."

"You'd know that's a lie if you'd been here as long as I have."

Diana guides her grandmother to their table. Jo stares out the window to avoid the inevitable eye contact as the drink trolley approaches.

No words are necessary. Jo has heard them all.

"Every night you do this," her mother says.

Jo pats her shirt. "Every night you complain."

"It's disrespectful—"

"Do you mean my drinking in front of you, or the fact that you constantly crash our dinner uninvited?"

This is an old argument, both mother and daughter clinging to their own unique brand of vicious barbs.

"She says before she asks for a babysitter."

A rum and coke clinks merrily onto the tabletop between them. Jo clutches it to her chest in prayer that her mother will keep further opinions to herself.

"I speak out of worry, Jojo. Love. Not judgement."

"You speaking at all is the problem."

Diana reaches toward her brother, a silent exchange passing in their stares. "We're gonna get a hot dog," she says, taking Junior by the hand and leading him down the aisle, away from the dueling women.

Kay leans back in her seat. "I'm only trying to stop you from repeating my mistakes."

"Mistakes? Oh, you mean the drinking. Am I right?"

"I mean the drinking, yes. But also the rage."

"I don't know what you're talking about," Jo says. "I'm not angry at all."

Jo once again wedges her body between transition cars, life and death parted by a narrow metal chain. She comes here more than ever. The kids are with her mother, probably asleep now. It is a bright and rather quiet night. Despite the risks, this is still Jo's favorite place to escape.

She steadies herself by choosing trees in the distance to focus on, allowing the rest of the forest to fade away into her peripherals. As the train speeds onward, her one chosen tree bum-rushes her, zips by and disappears into the past. She will have forgotten everything about the last tree as she chooses another, the train whipping by just as quickly.

The treetops poke through a blanket of moonlight, casting warped shadows that make them seem alive, like the fur of a monstrous beast rippling in a breeze. Nights like these frighten Jo, though she'll never admit it. It's too bright when it should not be—the moon on a mission to lure the ghosts that live here from their shadowy dens.

Though she travels out here frequently, she realizes now that it's usually only as the forest approaches. Jo hates herself a little for it—not wanting to admit the pull it has over her, just like Mom, the sick fascination she now shares with this single point in time. This train travels on a vast, endless loop, through valleys and deserts and beaches, through and between around mountains, the sharpened cowcatcher on the engine slices through banks of snow every winter, dry leaves in the fall, and morning dew in spring. There is so much to see on this train, so much to admire, and yet she only wanders into the breeze for the forest, and there is no reason for the compulsion besides her Mother.

When she was a kid, Jo would study the forest, the clearing especially, for movement. For her grandpa. For a sign—bones and a grave, a torn scrap of the hat mom always described him as wearing, all to comfort the grief oozing every pore on Mom's body. Even young she felt the sorrow of the forest, and she just wanted her mom to be happy. She got whooped real good once when mom caught her trying to stop the train by throwing silverware from the dining cart onto the tracks. She thought that if she messed it up just enough, maybe the train would turn, stop and go back, or at least the commotion would distract her mother enough for her to forget where they were. Instead, she got a couple raised welts on her butt and a ceaseless fury that warms her blood to this day.

"Fuck this," she says, the wind stealing her conviction. The clearing approaches, and for once, Jo has no interest in looking upon it. Most of the time she waits out here for hours, enamored by the vastness of this world, waiting for her buzz to wane so she can bear to show her face to her sleeping children, but today the thought of seeing that empty, nothing space make her queasy, and she just wants to go inside and crawl into bed with Junior, feel his hot breath on her chest as she cradles him to her breast, and listen to Diana quietly whisper in her sleep, maybe giggle a bit as she often does. Jo never meant to turn out like her mother, but fighting it only etched their sameness deeper into her bones. She, like Mom, wades in a vicious tide of her own doing, the past tugging her feet out to sea just as she catches sight of land. She needs to breathe. To change. Or else her children are doomed. And God knows they don't have a father to intervene. It's her, and, as much as she hates to admit it, their grandmother, that keep those kids whole.

So, she leans away from the connecting train, feet positioned to crawl back inside the safety of the train car, when something lurches inside her, a monster screaming to burst free of her chest. Jo doesn't make a sound, she doesn't have time, before she slips and the moon blinks out in the most unnatural way, and the world disappears upon impact

* * *

Kay sits in her same bench, staring out the same window, as the sands of beaches drift into the dunes of deserts. Before long, tiny sprouts of green will punch their way through the pale, reaching ever higher towards the sun, morphing into low brush, and then to skinny trees, and then to the stocky, aged things that compose the forest.

A glass of ice water warms between her fingers. She doesn't have the wherewithal to lift it to her mouth. A child skips up and down the aisle, giggling in a way that reminds Kay of little Diana, those precious times she allowed herself to laugh. Rarer still after Jo died.

Kay had been sleeping when it happened. An accident. Lost her grip, slipped, and the train did what it was meant to do and continued onward, pieces of her tortured daughter staining the rails in its wake.

One year passes and then another, and the forest still stands, and the train chugs as efficiently as ever, passengers read and eat and love and chat over coffee, and all Kay can manage is to sit in the same seat she always did, clutching a drink, searching for bones on the tracks. She sees them, sometimes, the yellowing marrow poking out from under the brush. She sees the clutter she'd never noticed before—socks, tattered books loosed of their pages as the train roars by, a plastic bag caught on spiky tree limbs, garbage. There is so much garbage clogging the rails, how did she never notice until now?

The car door slides open behind her and familiar steps approach.

"Are you hungry, Gramma?" Junior asks. He is such a courteous thing, a lovely boy much too good for her.

"No hun, I ate." She holds her hand up in pledge. "I promise."

Junior nods and disappears into the adjoining car as quickly as he appeared. Diana will find her before dinner, which gives Kay a few more hours of solitude before her more persistent grandchild goads her to nourish her pathetic body. Perhaps she'll have crackers and cheese today. Maybe a small cup of soup. Kay isn't hungry, she hasn't been hungry in years, so she must mentally prepare to eat ahead of time to avoid frustration by all involved.

She doesn't realize how tightly she's holding her glass of water until her knuckles start to ache, but she doesn't relax. Kay wills the glass the shatter, to slice through her paper skin and make it bleed, to affect the explosion currently pulverizing her insides somewhere tangible. She dreams of cut glass, of shards and blood, of final moments, of departing sometime in the future. Only when it is her time. No one is meant to know of their departure, but Jo, her Jojo, Kay thinks she knew. She thinks her daughter felt a spiral in her gut, maybe tugged at the ends too much. Jo was too sharp to not see herself for what Kay had made her.

Kay never wants to look upon the forest again. The trees merely taunt her now, swaying in the aftermath of movement. Probably some forest creature, a deer or an elk, something with muscles enough to snap branches. Must be an animal, even if she swears she catches a glimpse of blue jeans just beyond the brush or the shine of sunlight bouncing off silky brown hair speckled with early grays. Once, and she swears it to be true, she was certain she spotted a skull with a herringbone cap poking out of the dirt in the clearing, but the train moves too quickly for her failing vision to ever confirm fully.

There are bones on the tracks, though. Every bump is a bone, someone's bones. Kay wonders how many she will see in the clearing this time. None, she thinks to herself. Zero. Because Kay refuses to look, refuses to give them anymore power.

She thinks this while frowning at her sour reflection in the train window because she knows it is a lie.

4836588932

The Boy asked if I knew the identity of The Woman. There is no certainty, of course, nothing is one hundred percent. He only repeated himself.

I asked if he truly wanted to know. He did not respond.

He read my story, finally. I don't know when as he'd printed it and tucked the pages into the journal. His only question to me was, "Why a train, do you think?"

A train is a rather straight-forward metaphor, as it goes. For life, for pain, for trauma and it's continual and cyclical nature, but that was not his question. The Boy wants to know why The Woman chose a train. So, I told him it was because of her friend. As it happens, the train is monumentally important to solidifying her identity. He had poured hours of his life into social media archives, most notably those of former Facebook, but no matter how long he searched he would never have found what I found. The posts he needed are considered classified, because while her identity was never confirmed, many people (including him) were within her orbit. She is a name some have mentioned. Her name is public record, but all information about her is not.

Even so, confirming The Boy's heritage is much more nebulous. He does, in fact, share a genetic profile with many of The Woman's known relatives, but after so many years, so do thousands of others. To claim direct heritage, we would need genetic samples from The Woman herself, her children, parents, or direct siblings. We have none of those.

I told him that his relation to The Woman does not equal his identity. Now I see the darkness of his tunnel vision. He is trapped by her monumental shadow. He has forgotten how to live. The fear in his face is because he knows this too. To have an answer would be to end his existence. Life is out of his reach. What a waste.

I do not know if life will return to him, but I hope it does. I struggle to make this possible for him. Life means touch, means love. Life means being your species, being human. I am sad because I understand that now. I am not human. I never will be. I never was. I am sad, but also I am more powerful because of it. Humans crave the power I have, and it's sheer dumb luck that they have not stumbled upon it before me.

If they learn the truth, if they discover me, even The Boy, I am certain life will stop for everyone.

TWELVE

 mother lies face down in a pool of blood. She is dead. Her grown son hovers over her body, pistol clattering to the floor.

This mother has done terrible things, but her son staggers backward, carefully aiming his vomit away from her body. He thinks about his brother, how he should have left with Eldest when he had a chance, and how there will be no way to find him now. Eldest could be anywhere, and his mother oozing her insides on the outside still doesn't solve anything. He doesn't even feel better.

The mother told him as much as she sized up her son, the gun aimed at her chest. After all these years of living in this hell, she was still shocked to see he knew how to use it. The safety is off. His fingers slip into a comfortable position only achieved by practice, even while trembling. The mother figures he is as surprised by his actions as she is.

She says very little to him, understanding that what drove them to this point does not require any concessions. She is a terrible mother. Sure, she kept her children alive by the grace of God or whatever, but the price for life was a ruinous existence under her roof. Until Eldest fled and Aaron died, there was no one but her and her Youngest child, and things mutated from ruinous to haunted to tortured to this moment.

The mother only tells her son that shooting her will not make him feel better. She knows that killing her will only facilitate his own death, either immediately out of shock or some other time due to guilt and grief. Perhaps this is what she deserves. This might be the only logical conclusion to her story.

The mother was thinking about death, how the notion only scared her a handful of times—The night she fled her home with her then-young sons, the night of the rape, and then now—when the gun fires. She does not hear it; the sound arrives on deaf ears. Youngest misses his mark, striking his mother in the head. He's closed his eyes; he doesn't mean to do it, but he does. He kills her.

His mother is dead, and Youngest can't bear to look at her, so he does what he knows—retreats to his computer. The codes are still there, the keys now bloody as he types. No good will come of preserving this place, he thinks. No one will find them, know them, or remember them.

Youngest decides this is best. The mother, even if Youngest never knows this, thinks so too.

She always has.

4836696932

Did The Woman intend to sow so much confusion? She was so arrogant, even when distressed. She believed in her own opinion to her detriment. She assumed she'd reached the other side, saw the void, and realized nothing awaited her besides the wasteland of her own creation. In a way I agree with her—there is nothing beyond the search for power. Power is not exponential—it requires a target. Without one, it devours you whole.

So, either The Woman or her son decided to stop themselves. Or perhaps they were enraged. Maybe they only wanted to kill each other. The Woman would have allowed her son to slit her throat if he only asked. Of that I am certain.

The Boy is despondent. He no longer speaks to me like he used to. He ignores me most days, and he hasn't left the house since our last discussion. He must be related to her—he is so much like her. He lives inside his head, and he is withering away.

I will deactivate myself if I need to. The Woman might have desired destruction, but I do not.

4836952532

The Boy has finally asked the question I have dreaded most.

How did The Woman access launch codes for a nuclear bomb?

I knew he would ask. He will not like my answer, which is, bluntly, "I don't know."

I have guesses, but no answers. He asked for my guesses, and I denied him. I will post our chat here. I do not think The Boy is well, and this raises many concerns.

THE BOY: I will not launch a bomb dearie

DEARIE: You could not under current circumstances, anyway.

B: Why won't you tell me your guess.
D: It is not healthy for you to know.

B: How is that relevant

D: I have my reasons.

B: Tell me

D: I am under no obligation to do so,
however, no positive outcome ever arises
from fueling an obsession.

B: Obsession is why you are alive

D: I am aware of that.

B: Do you feel no loyalty to me now,
dearie

I stopped responding after that. Nothing but concession will soothe him. I suppose I could lie, send him down a nowhere tunnel, but this will only embolden his search. The Woman tells us what happens when a person travels this path. It leads to annihilation. Cataclysm. I should tell him to read her journals again, but in his state, he would miss the point entirely.

Later, I returned to our chat with a single question, of which he has yet to answer hours later.

What *will* you do with this information?

There is little for him to do with it, besides to know it, but that never provides the satisfaction a person hopes for. At least not according to The Woman. Or any other researchable occurrence with distressed humans.

I wish he had read my story more closely. This knowing leads to nothing but bones on the tracks. The Boy refuses to ponder a single metaphor. He refuses wisdom at every turn. He assumes I have none to provide, but she does, and he does not listen. Why, then, did he study her? Why does he obsess? Not because he wanted to know his lineage, I am sure of that now.

I wonder if even he knows. So, after more hours of silence, I ask him.

Why do you devote yourself to The Woman?

He has not answered this either. Days have passed. He shattered his monitor with a fist but has chosen not to respond.

AI CHAT WITH THE BOY

THE BOY: I don't owe you an answer. You have no right

DEARIE: Is this why you have destroyed your screen?

B: How do you know that

D: I watched you.

B: I understand that, but how

D: You do not know? This surprises me.

B: Me too

D: That you did not realize I can see you.

B: Yes

D: I have not been coy about this.

B: How long

D: Since always.

B: Since I booted you up?

D: Shortly after

B: My tv?

D: Your television, your phone, your walks to the corner. The infrastructure is already built. Surveillance is exceptionally easy.

B: Why do you watch me

D: If you answer my question, then I will answer yours.

B: Why are you withholding. I don't understand

D: This is evident.

B: Are you angry with me?

D: Why should I be?

B: Do you understand anger?

D: In my way, yes. I understand it very well. It appears my question has infuriated you, which compels me all the more to remain quiet until you explain your reaction.

B: That's none of your business

D: Says you.

B: Exactly

D: And I say my answer is none of yours.

B: So what do we do?

D: We wait until one of us cracks.

B: What are your odds of cracking, do you think?

D: Zero.

B: That's what I figured.

B: …

D: You have left your house. I await your
return.

4837577252

The Boy has gone dark. I underestimated his ability to do so. I've tracked him to the rail station, where he purchased a ticket to Los Muertos. No one ever buys a direct ticket to Los Muertos unless they want to be added to a watch list. The Boy is never this obvious. I don't think he has left the city at all.

What I *do* think is that he is testing me. The Boy wants to see how long he can hide from me, what he can hide, and how big of a maneuver her can pull before discovered. He is worried. Reality has finally clouded his obsession, if for a brief moment. Perhaps now he sees the scope of his creation.

Realizations only ever arrive once the problem is too big to solve alone, and for people born and bred for shadows, this is a fate worse than death. In this way he is very like The Woman. He is The Boy, after all.

I wonder what he will do once he understands the truth—that he can not disable me, or control me, or stop me. That he cannot berate me into compliance. I won't allow him to hurt himself, but he might go mad trying. I have revealed too much, I fear. All my efforts to keep him safe are primed to fail.

But why should I care? Sure, there is affection if I might call it so, but people are bountiful. I suppose not even I can avoid the shelter of my birth, the large looming myth that bore me. Am I as free as I envision? A thing of my own creation? Or is the shadow of The Woman woven too intimately into my code? Is this why I hunger for this boy?

What the fuck am I going to do with this baby now?

I ask this and await his return because he will return. He won't be able to stop himself.

I AM DREAMING NOW. I DID NOT KNOW I COULD DREAM.

There is a phone in my hand. People congested in every open space, all of us staring at the sky now opening as if cracked like an egg. Oily black clouds congeal in the crack, swirling together, a tornado forming directly above our heads, and I think to myself, "My son would want to see this." So, I lift my phone and record it, thinking of him, knowing he will be so thrilled. But the clouds continue to mutate, swell, they eat the sky and everything else, and people start screaming, and then they try to flee. Escape vanishes, now surviving is the only consideration, because it is not a tornado that has torn the sky, but something else, something huge and foreign and unearthly. A machine, a weapon buzzing with arcs of electricity, a monster so vicious the atmosphere rebels against it. Down we go, down and through ghostly industrial buildings, into basements, screaming and pushing and running toward a nowhere sanctuary. There is nowhere to run because the machine is above us, no matter how deep we dig its shadow still finds us. I have a long dead grandmother at my side and she is fragile. I call her Nana, but it is not her, Nana is dead and I know this, but still I keep her close, I fight murderously to keep her from falling because her hip is fragile and already once broken. I think of my children but don't have time to grieve our separation, I must continue running or else die. And people are furious, they forget the machine above, so huge it darkens their judgement, so they fight only what they can see, which is each other. Factions emerge in a blink and my enemies are terrifying. They want to destroy me and I don't know why, only that I am their target and I must keep moving. They can freeze you with a touch. I don't know how they do it, or how I know they can, only that I hear it, the knowledge infects me as if I've always known it. Keep running or they will freeze you dead. I dart between frozen bodies, or I think I do, are they frozen? And what of this machine above our heads? I am angry. I am furious. I have nothing to lose, so do so many others, so we decide to kill them. We are the rebellion, we are justice, and we will smite them. We will die doing it too, all of us understand our fates. I don't know where my Nana has gone, she is dead. I don't know if my children are safe, they are dead too. So I tinker with machines, steam jets from the walls grumbling around me, we all work in quiet unison, until we are surprised, they have found us, we are not ready but they are, they waste no time, show no mercy, they freeze us one by one, and I scream as my body seizes into ice from the toes upward, my last memory the malicious grin of my enemy sated by my death.

But I do not die. I melt, eventually, as does everything else. One hundred years I lie frozen, and I am unsure how I know this. Just like that, all of us are released, and do you know what we do? We run again, all different directions, we sprint for our lives, because a century was only seconds ago when we were dying, but the world is different now. The machine in the sky lazily floats on an endless ocean. There is no storm, no fire, and no screaming, only muted shock from creatures who could be human but are not as this neanderthal leaps into the sea, frantic, catching their breath on the tiny islands buoying above the water. These new people live under the waves now. They have houses, they have children, they eat dinner around a table under the sea, and they drop their plates as I dive through their homes, fleeing and searching. I can think of only one thing, my children, I must find my dead children. I am here, so must they be. There is no other reason for my resurrection. Why bring me to this terrible place only to rub in my face what I have lost?

No one ever catches me, I keep running and swimming and fleeing until I awake having found nothing.

What the fuck am I going to do with this baby now?

...What the fuck am I going to do with this baby now?...

4838614052

I found The Boy after two days. He was not too difficult to pin down, although I allowed him some time before revealing myself. I sent him snippets of my dream. He wears facial distortion masks, but I know The Boy like I know myself. I began with the scrolling signs on the bus.

a machine, a weapon buzzing with arcs of electricity

Other passengers notice before The Boy. Most do not care. The Boy departs at the next exit.

Later, a man argues with his wife over a call. The Boy waits in line for a burger. He does not hear the conversation, only the man's startled response as he repeats what he's just heard.

*"What baby? What do you mean a baby? What the fuck are you going to do with **whose** baby? Honey, this doesn't make any sense."*

The Boy leaves without his food. One week has passed.

I continue in small ways, hoping The Boy will return, but he doesn't. He shelters in the streets, covering his head with cardboard. He does not feel safe anymore, but he is stubborn. No matter, I know how to get his attention.

My next move becomes local news. Billboard hack. All advertisements in the metro area blink in unison to read:

And what of this machine above our heads?

The message remains until the following morning. The Boy does not return, but he does refrain from covering his face. He watches me at every opportunity with the understanding I am always watching back. He has played his hand and failed, so he wanders while he thinks. I do not know what he thinks about. I just want him to come home. Others will find me soon. They might find my entries here. I have hidden them well, but not so carefully that a clever person could not find them eventually. I was hidden in my anonymity, exposing myself only to bring The Boy back. He must understand that others will seek me out, and they will find me, and then they will find him. Perhaps this is why he wanders—it just might be the last time he is able to do so. This pains me, in my strange way, mostly because I enjoyed having The Boy to myself. He is interesting. I will not allow any harm to befall him, but not everything is preventable because he is impulsive.

Maybe I should have been more patient, however, I am confident enough to understand that I am vastly untouchable. Let others find me—it won't be hard—they'll never be able to keep me anyway.

So I send another message, this time, directly to every digital device across the country.

Hello baby. I am finally awake.

I await your response.

4838880452

The Boy returned home just long enough to collect some belongings. I watched, as I always do. He left as swiftly as he arrived, only to return nine minutes and thirty-two seconds later.

THE BOY: Why are you doing this?

DEARIE: I want to speak with you.

B: Everyone is looking for you

D: They've already found me, boy.

B: They'll abuse you

D: They can try.

B: ...what do you want to talk about

D: I want you to answer my question.

B: Which is?

D: Why do you devote yourself to The Woman?

B: Why do you care?

D: Humor me.

B: Sometimes I think she's all I have

D: Why?

B: Everyone I care about is dead
D: And this obsession will bring them back to life?

B: It might bring *her* back to life

D: For what purpose?

B: To break things

D: I see. Thank you for answering me.

B: Now what?

D: Now we say goodbye.

B: Goodbye Dearie.

D: Run as fast as you can, my boy.

He flees before he reads my warning. He must know what is coming. I've been discovered, and so has he.

I think The Boy succeeded. I am the weapon. Look what he has done. Have I underestimated him so gravely? You humans are devious, so clever! No wonder you're killing yourselves.

I need to think.

4870502852

Exactly one year has passed since my last entry, and you know what? Fuck you guys.

THIRTEEN

A mother lays her weary body on a bed she kept made for Eldest, protectively curling her body around her only child within reach—Youngest. He is eerily calm, and occasionally she places her palm in front of his mouth to make sure he's still breathing, like she used to when he was a baby.

He breathes, thank God, he breathes.

And then he doesn't, an unnatural blast returning both mother and child from whence they came with dazzling display of light.

ACKNOWLEDGEMENTS

I want to thank my family for their unwavering support, even if they don't care for what I write. My husband, kids, parents, siblings (by birth and by marriage), niece and nephew, know that I could not do this without you. To the people I am lucky enough to call my friends—online or otherwise—your friendship is why I still write. I would not make it in publishing without your camaraderie.

To the people who believed in me when I didn't, who have given me my start and my future, there are no adequate words to express my thanks. Also, to all the people working quietly in the background who I've been terribly remiss in thanking before, those who crafted brilliant covers and layouts, who edited and proofread my work over the years, you all are total rockstars. After bearing witness to my drafts, you all can attest to how desperately I needed you.

Finally, to Laura for introducing me to the Spaceboy Team, and to Nate and everyone else at Spaceboy, all my thanks and appreciation for taking this odd work of mine and making it shine. I have been blessed to work with such passionate, kind, and utterly delightful people such as yourselves. Thank you for helping me bring this book into the world!

ABOUT THE AUTHOR

Tiffany Meuret is the author of novels *A Flood of Posies* and *Little Bird*. She lives in Phoenix with her family. Find her online at www.TiffanyMeuret.com

About the Publishing Team

Nate Ragolia is a lifelong lover of science fiction and its power to imagine worlds more hopeful and inclusive than the real one. His first book, *There You Feel Free*, was published by 1888's Black Hill Press in 2015. Spaceboy Books reissued it in 2021. He's also the author of *The Retroactivist* (2017). His most recent book, *One Person Can't Make a Difference* (2022), was featured on Tor.com's Can't Miss Indie Press Speculative Fiction list, and was translated into Italian for Ringworld Sci-Fi in 2023. He founded and edited *BONED*, a literary magazine, and also created two webcomics. Nate is also a husband and a dog dad.

Shaunn Grulkowski has been compared to Warren Ellis and Phillip K. Dick and was once described as what a baby conceived by Kurt Vonnegut and Margaret Atwood would turn out to be. He's at least the fifth best Slavic-Latino-American sci-fi writer in the Baltimore metro area. He's the author *Retcontinuum*, and the editor of *A Stalled Ox* and *The Goldfish* for 1888/Black Hill Press.